"It won't work, M you're a tumblewe **it," Rolph said.**

"No," she said. She meant to say, _____ longer, but his hands were caressing her shoulders and back, warm through the fabric of her blouse. She sighed and lifted her head, letting her hair fall down over her back. With an impatient gesture, he gathered her hair and flipped it out of his way. Then he astounded her, thrilled her by stroking his hand slowly and sensuously down over the twist of hair that lay across her shoulder and chest.

"Your hair—" She heard him swallow hard, then felt his hands leave her skin. "It feels like satin," he said. "And it smells . . . good." For just an instant he touched it again, as if he couldn't help himself.

She was melting inside as she half turned and gazed at him. "Does it?"

He licked his lips. With one hand under her chin, he tilted her head back and stared down at her. His green eyes were luminous and filled with desire, as well as confusion and doubt. "Yes, it does."

"Rolph . . ." Her voice was little more than a whisper when she reached up and touched his jaw.

"When did you get so beautiful?" he asked huskily, surprising her.

"I don't know I . . . didn't know I was." Men had told her she was, but she'd never believed it—until now.

"You are," he said, his mouth a breath away from hers. He was going to kiss her. Or she was going to faint from wanting it. . . .

WHAT ARE *LOVESWEPT* ROMANCES?

They are stories of true romance and touching emotion. We believe those two very important ingredients are constants in our highly sensual and very believable stories in the *LOVESWEPT* line. Our goal is to give you, the reader, stories of consistently high quality that may sometimes make you laugh, sometimes make you cry, but are always fresh and creative and contain many delightful surprises within their pages.

Most romance fans read an enormous number of books. Those they truly love, they keep. Others may be traded with friends and soon forgotten. We hope that each *LOVESWEPT* romance will be a treasure—a "keeper." We will always try to publish

LOVE STORIES YOU'LL NEVER FORGET
BY AUTHORS YOU'LL ALWAYS REMEMBER

The Editors

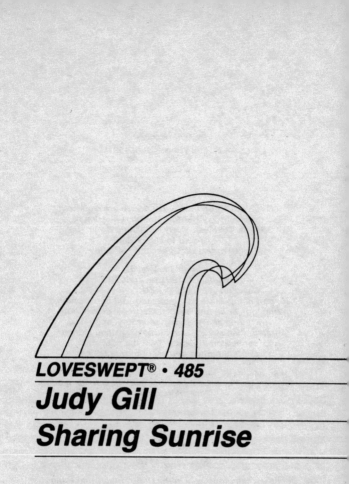

LOVESWEPT® • 485

Judy Gill

Sharing Sunrise

 BANTAM BOOKS
NEW YORK • TORONTO • LONDON • SYDNEY • AUCKLAND

SHARING SUNRISE

A Bantam Book / July 1991

*If you would be interested in receiving protective vinyl
covers for your Loveswept books, please write to this address
for information:*

*Loveswept
Bantam Books
P.O. Box 985
Hicksville, NY 11802*

ISBN 0-553-44160-4

Published simultaneously in the United States and Canada

PRINTED IN THE UNITED STATES OF AMERICA

OPM   0 9 8 7 6 5 4 3 2 1

One

Marian Crane glared at the sign on the door—
Jeanie Leslie, Career Consultants—as she
stormed into the office. She ignored the startled
young woman who looked up from her typewriter, and ignored her bitten-off question.
Shoving open the door to Jeanie's private office,
she said, "Do me one big favor!"

"What's that?" Jeanie McKenzie, née Leslie,
asked.

"Find Rolph McKenzie, marina operator, boat
broker, and egomaniac, an assistant who'll sab-
otage his business, sink his boat, and break his
heart."

Jeanie grimaced. "Turned you down, huh? I
was afraid of that. The trouble is, he thinks he
can do it all on his own. But those of us who
know him and care for him realize he can't, and
that he's making himself ill trying."

"He turned me down all right," Marian exclaimed. "And insulted me in the bargain."

"Sorry, kiddo," Jeanie said with a sigh. "I shouldn't have let Max talk me into sending you. But he was worried about his brother. I don't blame you for being hurt."

"I'm not hurt, I'm mad!" Marian slammed her bright red purse onto Jeanie's desk and flung herself into a chair. After kicking off her red shoes, she lifted one foot onto the opposite knee and rubbed it. "I'm so mad I've spent the past hour walking, hoping to burn off some of it, but it just keeps getting bigger and bigger inside me until I want to explode!"

"You're hurt," Jeanie said decisively, "and I would be too. What did he say?"

"That he didn't want some butterfly-brain who didn't know a halyard from a half hitch!"

Jeanie pursed her lips and swiped a hand over her messy bush of uncontrollable hair. "Oh! Okay, I agree. You're mad." She sat back, folded her hands, and cocked her head to one side. "Where to, now?"

Marian shrugged and massaged the other foot. "I don't know. Maybe the Sorbonne? What about the Australian outback? Or Antarctica. I've never been there."

"Quitting? Giving up?"

"Maybe. What's the use? He can't . . . see me. I mean, he looks at me and sees me at fourteen, with skintight jeans and hair in my eyes and six earrings in each ear. Dammit, Jeanie, I went down there today meaning to be seen as an adult. Look at me! A perfectly businesslike suit, accessories that match, a no-nonsense hair style, subtle but effective makeup and perfume, and what do I get? He tousled my hair! He called me 'kitten'! He as good as told me to run along and play with my dollies because he had *women* coming in to interview for jobs. He treated me the way he has since I was three years old—like the kid next door."

Angrily, she plucked pins from her blond hair and let it swing down around her shoulders, then shook her head to spread it out.

"Oh, I was noticed all right," she went on. "One man dripped white paint all over his toes, to say nothing of his teak deck. Another one dropped his screwdriver overboard. I got more whistles than at a truck stop and eyeballs roved along the wharf after me. But from my good old friend Rolph McKenzie, what did I get? Mussed-up hair and a belly laugh!" Her voice cracked as she added, "He didn't mean to hurt my feelings. He's simply so used to teasing me, he doesn't know when to quit. And the funny part is, I think he did notice me—as a woman. He looked, well, I have to say 'stunned' for a second or two when I first walked into his office. Then it was as if somebody had pushed a button and reminded him that the woman in the white shantung suit was, after all, only little Marian. Dammit, that wasn't the button I wanted to push!"

Jeanie would have laughed if it hadn't been for the wobble in Marian's voice showing how close the younger woman was to tears. "Tell me what happened," she said gently.

Marian pulled a face. "At first, it looked pretty good. I mean, he showed me around his new office and home complex." She shook her head. "Three weeks he's lived there and he doesn't have any furniture in his home besides a desk and a bed. The offices are fully furnished, though. Anyway, he told me how he'd had to battle every city ordinance and even the port authority before they let him build a structure on pilings out there in the middle of the marina, and then he asked why I'd come. I told him you'd sent me down for an interview.

"That was when I got the belly laugh. He reminded me that I'd failed typing twice in school and had never got into shorthand because of that, and even suggested I'd be useless in the office because I can't make coffee. He did concede, though, that I have a nice phone manner."

Jeanie bit a pencil. "Didn't you tell him you weren't looking for office work?"

"Yes, and he laughed again and said I couldn't be serious. When I told him I was, he said"—Marian dropped her voice an octave and looked down her nose at Jeanie—"'Marian, you haven't been serious a day in your entire life. You've been a professional student, flitting from school to school, from country to country, from job to job.'" Marian scowled. "For a minute, I thought he was going to say 'from man to man,' as well, but luckily for him, he didn't. He simply reminded me that I hadn't held any job for very long and asked me what, exactly, I thought I was qualified for."

Marian swallowed hard, remembering how she'd felt when he said that. She couldn't deny any of it, because it was true. She had spent too many years wandering, studying, becoming an education junkie, and had ended up well qualified for no one thing and overqualified for too many things. "I told him that you thought I'd work well in the boat brokerage business and that Max agreed."

Jeanie frowned. "Was that wise, do you think, bringing Max in?"

Marian shrugged. "I don't know. I didn't mention Max's threat to pull his investment capital out of Rolph's business if he didn't hire me. If I'm to get a job, I want it to be on my own, not because somebody threatens somebody else. I told Rolph I really needed a job, and since it was obvious he really needed assistance, it was only sensible that two old friends help each other out."

"He wasn't buying, huh?"

"Not for a minute." Marian shook her head, remembering how Rolph had raised his brows and asked, "Need? Why do you 'need' a job?"

"For one thing, I like to eat," she'd replied tartly. "I like to pay the rent."

He had blinked in surprise. "Your parents charge you rent?"

Looking at Jeanie, Marian said, "He thought I was still living at home, for heaven's sake, thought my parents still supported me. He even suggested I could walk dogs for the SPCA! The man has no concept of reality, not when it applies to me. So to give him a little dose of that reality, I practically flung my résumé in his face and insisted he read it. Or else he'd be in contravention of his contract with you."

Jeanie grinned. "Good for you. And?"

Marian released a short, angry puff of air. "He was favorably impressed. Actually he was nearly speechless when he realized I hadn't been goofing off all those years, but had a bachelor's degree in sociology and a more than passing acquaintance with six foreign languages." She smiled wryly. "And he was gratifyingly bug-eyed over my MBA."

"But?" Jeanie prompted, sitting forward in her chair, her brows drawn together. "He didn't pull that 'need a man for the job' garbage, did he?" Marian's expression was enough of an answer. She said, "I'll hang him by his—He knows that's illegal!"

"It wasn't that so much as he wants somebody he can trust to stay on and get the job done," Marian said. "And he doesn't think I'm that person. I have to admit that my past performance suggests I might flit away, but that was the past. This is now. I even told him that I have to stay in Victoria because, while my mom may be better now, she and Dad are both getting on. I want to be close by in case something else happens. Dammit, Jeanie, I practically begged him to give me a chance, let me try to prove myself for two months, then he could make a final decision. That was when he said he needed a guy who was in for the long haul, not some ditzy dame who didn't know a halyard from a half hitch, at which point I walked out on him. He can take his damned brokerage and marina and st—"

"Jeanie, have you heard from—" Rolph strode into Jeanie's office, then halted when he saw Marian. His gaze swept over her flushed, angry face. "Oh," he said. "You're here." With a pained, helpless glance at Jeanie, he crouched before Marian, tucking a strand of her hair back behind one of her ears. "Hey," he said, when she shook his hand off, "I came to tell you I'm sorry. I acted like a jerk, and what I said was insulting, though I didn't mean it to be. I thought I was being funny. Forgive me?"

"Of course," she said in a frigid tone, half turning from him, her hair curtaining her face. She got to her feet. "I'll leave you and Jeanie to discuss strategy for the continued search for

Rolph McKenzie's perfect assistant, should *he* even exist." She glanced around for her friend, and was surprised to discover she wasn't there.

"The search is over," he said. "I hired the first secretary who came this morning and told her to choose an aide for herself out of the ones who came after."

Marian's temper flared. "How nice for her. Can she type? Can she file? How's her telephone manner?"

"I didn't ask. I figured if Jeanie sent her to me, she was worth hiring. "I . . . trust Jeanie's judgment."

"No kidding." Marian turned over her left shoe with her toes and stepped into it, then found her right shoe and donned that, too, giving herself the advantage of a few more inches of height. Still, she couldn't meet Rolph's gaze. She was afraid that if she looked too long at his strong, handsome face, his compelling green eyes, he would know that her hurt didn't stem entirely from his not hiring her. He'd realize that she was hurt by his inability to see her as a woman—especially since she so very clearly saw him as a man. Keeping her head turned from his sharp gaze, she gathered her pins from Jeanie's desk and let them trickle from her hand into her purse.

"No kidding," he murmured. "I trust her judgment about you, too, Marian. I want you to come work with me."

Slowly, she turned. Just as slowly, she lifted her gaze to his face. After several moments, she said again with utterly no expression, "No kidding."

His mouth twisted up at one corner. "Oh, hell," he said. "You told me you'd forgiven me."

She snapped her purse closed. "I lied."

"Marian . . ."

Without another word she walked out of the office, quietly closing the door behind her.

He caught up with her just as the elevator arrived and got in with her. "What do I have to do?" he asked. "Grovel?"

She considered that. "It might help."

"I'm groveling. I'm abject. Forgive me."

She continued to ponder, her chin on her fist. Finally, she nodded. "I'll try. You'll buy me lunch?"

The elevator stopped and they stepped out. Rolph grinned. "I'll buy you lunch every day for the rest of the month."

"If what?"

"If you forgive me."

She raised her brows. "And?"

He sighed. "And come to work at the marina."

Her smile was radiant. For an instant, Rolph felt its impact deep inside where he was most a man. Like a tiderip it came at him unexpectedly and rattled his rigging. With difficulty, he clamped down on it. This was Marian, for heaven's sake, he told himself. He couldn't go responding to her the way he did to a datable woman.

It just wouldn't be right.

"For a two-month trial period," he added.

"Okay," she said. "It's a deal."

"Shake." He reached out to enfold her hand in his, and was surprised to discover she was trembling slightly. Hell, the poor kid really *had* wanted the job, he thought. Oh, well, what were two months out of the whole scope of his life? He'd let her stay that long. By then, maybe even before, she'd be tired of it. Marian Crane had never stuck with anything.

Look at her now, he told himself. The last time he'd seen her, her hair had been red and her eyes blue. Now, she was a green-eyed blond. Next week, she'd probably be a brown-eyed brunette, and the month after that, who knows? All he knew was she'd probably be gone, and he could get on with finding the right man—person—for the job. And get over this extraordinary response his body persisted in having in her subtle yet unforgettable scent.

Max might think it was his phone call that had gotten Marian the job. He might believe it was his veiled threat to withdraw his investment capital if Rolph didn't hire Marian—or someone—to take up the slack and hence protect Max's investment. He didn't need to know, nobody needed to know, that Rolph's mind had been made up by nothing more than the sheen of tears he'd glimpsed in Marian's eyes just before she stormed out of his office. That, and the indelible memory of one moment of forbidden enchantment, when he'd seen her walking toward him in the bright morning sun.

Now, curling an arm over her shoulders, he led her to where he had parked his car.

"Okay," he said, "where does my new assistant want to go for lunch?"

"Why don't you pick up a couple of sandwiches for us?" she suggested, shrugging his arm off and turning to her own car, parked three slots over. "I'll meet you at the office and we can eat while we talk about business."

Clearly, Rolph thought, if he suddenly found Marian enchanting, she found him less so. She didn't even want his arm around her shoulders, though it had been there a hundred times before.

That was the way it should be, he told himself as he got into his car. Businesslike. Cool. Controlled. Because not only was Marian his employee, she was an old family friend. A smart guy didn't mess around with a relationship like that. Especially a smart guy who wanted some permanence in his life. The last thing he needed was to be attracted to a top-drawer, well-bred, first-class . . . hobo.

"You've been contracting out interior design on the refit jobs, haven't you?" Marian asked, brushing bread crumbs from her lap. This was their ninth working lunch in the nearly two weeks of Marian's employment. True to his promise, Rolph had bought lunch for her every day.

He looked up from a report he was writing. "Yes, but since we're a brokerage business, not a shipyard, I contract out the entire refit. It only makes sense. Why have someone on staff who can do interior design?"

"But you do have. Me. When I was in New Zealand I worked for a company that did offshore yacht interiors."

He gave her a startled look. "You? I've seen your apartment, remember? All zebra stripes and spears, with boars' heads sticking out of the walls."

Marian shuddered at the memory. "That was when I was in college, for goodness' sake! I was nineteen years old and going through an African phase. My tastes have changed." She crossed one leg over the other, swinging her neatly shod foot. "Haven't yours over the years? Didn't you like things ten years ago that you now think are outrageous, and vice versa?"

"I suppose so," he said, then grinned at a memory. "Make that definitely. Ten years ago I was in love with a woman whose only expression of emotion, be it satisfaction or disgust or pleasure or pain, was a faint, weak little 'wow . . .' I thought she was fantastic because of all she could convey with that one word. That was before I figured out that it constituted nearly her entire vocabulary."

"Hmm," Marian said. "And what are your tastes in women today?"

He shrugged. "Oh, I don't know. It's hard to put something like that into words."

"Pretend you're writing a personal ad."

He stared at her. Did she know he'd done just that on two occasions? No. Of course she didn't. He wondered what she would say if she did know. Would she laugh at him? Pity him? He didn't want to find out.

"Wanted," he began, "SF, sexy, cheerful, eager for new experiences. Must like outdoors, sailing, hiking, skiing. Some culture okay."

Marian giggled. "*Some* culture?"

"You know, a bit intellectual, but not overdone. I'd hate to spend all my time in museums and art galleries or attending the symphony, though those are fine sometimes. And she'd need to like books and movies, but not just highbrow stuff. The real things that real people read and enjoy. Spy stories, mysteries, romance, adventure. You know. Escapism."

"So a brainy woman is out."

"I didn't say that. There's nothing wrong with intelligent women. I'd just prefer one who didn't take herself too seriously all the time. I like a woman with a mind of her own, one who doesn't let other people make decisions for her." He hesitated, drawing his brows together. "Unless they're the right decisions, of course."

"Of course," Marian said dryly. "Such as the ones you'd make for her."

He laughed shortly. "I guess you're right about that. But I believe most women secretly like the idea of a man being the man, being in charge, at least of some things. You know, I'll be the captain, you be the mate."

"You Tarzan, she Jane?"

"Something like that. Not that it matters. I don't think my ideal woman exists, and if she did, she wouldn't want me."

Marian stared at him. "What do you mean, she wouldn't want you?"

He shrugged. "I've never had much success with women. They never stay interested for long. I guess I don't know what they want."

She had to laugh. "I understand Freud had that same problem."

"You think I'm joking."

"I know you're joking! Rolph, don't forget, I've watched the stream of women going in and out of the McKenzie family home all my life. You've never been short of dates."

"Hah! That 'stream' of women was there for Max, not me. I was lucky sometimes and got the leftovers, but all Max ever had to do was give a little wink and a gesture, and they raced away from me toward him."

Marian couldn't believe what she was hearing, but Rolph's expression told her he believed it.

"I thought it would get better when Max was married," he continued musingly, "but all that did was stop the women coming around, period."

"Hey, come on," she said. "You don't have to wait for them to come around, Rolph. They're out there. All you have to do is go out and find them." Good heavens, what was she doing? Marian asked herself. Sending him out on a woman-hunt when she was sitting right there, his for the taking?

"It's not that easy," he said. "I have this notion of my ideal woman and, like I said, I'm not sure she's real. But what about you?" he asked. "What kind of man are you looking for?"

Tall, lean, blond, and green-eyed, she answered silently. Somewhat blind when it comes to what's good for him. Stupid, you could say, about some things, things that should be staring him right in the face.

"What makes you think I'm looking for a man?" she countered.

"Every single woman is looking for a man." His tone was impatient, as if he were stating the obvious.

"I've been married."

He rolled his eyes. "I remember. You broke your parents' hearts with that little escapade. Eloping while you were in college and then spending only six weeks with the guy. What kind of marriage was that, anyway?"

"One that taught me a great deal."

"Like what?"

"That he was much too old for me, that some of the things he thought were normal I found disgusting, and that my taste in men was as lousy as my judgment."

"I assume that must have changed in the

what . . . three, four years since you were married?"

She shook her head. How come she had paid so much attention to his life, when he had no idea what hers was all about? "Eight years, Rolph! I was twenty. He was twenty-eight. We were worlds apart, even in—"

"You were too young!" Rolph interrupted. He had to shut her up. He didn't want to hear about her sex life with that creep she'd married. Just thinking about it filled him with pain and a terrible kind of rage.

"I wasn't too young," she said. "Lots of women marry younger than twenty and stay married for sixty years. Wendell and I simply weren't compatible. And yes, of course my taste and judgment have both changed." She frowned, rubbing her forehead with her fingertips, then added quietly, "But I'm not certain that means they're any better, either of them."

Rolph was surprised and touched by the genuine uncertainty in her voice. "You're young and beautiful," he said gruffly. "You shouldn't have any trouble finding the right guy."

His compliment took her breath away. Did he really think she was beautiful? She wanted to ask, but instead said breezily, "Maybe not, except that my boss makes it difficult."

Rolph stiffened, then walked a few feet away to straighten a framed lithograph of Earle G. Barlow's *White Ghost* on the wall. "I didn't mean to make things difficult for you," he said, turning to face her. "But we had to meet with those clients that evening."

Right, Marian thought. And since it was the first and only time Rolph had taken her along to a client meeting, she couldn't help but believe it was because he didn't want her to go out with Kevin Durano.

"Durano's not your type," he said. "Talk about too old for you! The guy's forty-five, has been married three times, and likes to think of himself as a playboy. The interior of his boat is latter-day decadent and he hasn't had it out of the marina in years."

"I don't know if he's my type or not, but he did say that when he got back from the business trip he's on, he'd like to take me to Estevan's."

Rolph's eyes narrowed, and he strode over to her desk. "The hell he did!"

Marian hid a pleased smile at this little show of jealousy. "Why shouldn't he? It's reportedly the top place in town for seafood and, as a private club, it's hard to get into. The waiting list for memberships is a mile long. Even with his membership, Kevin told me, he sometimes has to wait days for a table. I'm looking forward to dinner there. I understand they have a great dance band."

"Fine. Then that's where we'll take the Mastersons when they're in town tomorrow. I hold a membership, a charter membership," he continued pointedly, "so I can get reservations with only a day's notice."

He looked positively fierce, and Marian's heartbeat quickened. "The Mastersons?" she managed to ask.

"Clients. They're flying in from Barbados to look at a couple of boats we have listed, *Windrider* and *Neo Cleo*. It'll be too late when they arrive to show them around, so I plan to wine and dine them, let them sleep on the information I'll regale them with, then take them over both boats in the morning when they're feeling well-rested."

"And when the tide's high," she murmured.

He smiled. "You have been paying attention, haven't you?"

"Of course. I have an excellent teacher who makes every aspect of the business interesting. Paying attention to you is no hardship, Rolph."

He gazed at her thoughtfully for a moment. "Thank you," he said, and reached out to run the backs of his fingers down her cheek. "That's nice to hear." While her heart went still in her chest, he stroked her cheek again. "And you're nice to touch," he said softly. Suddenly, he jerked his hand back and shook his head rapidly. "I mean, teach. You're easy to teach. You learn quickly and well."

She swallowed hard. "Thanks," she said, then stared down at her desk. When she looked up again, Rolph was hard at work at his own desk. Her chin on her fist, she gazed at his quarter-profile, wondering why he had stopped touching her just when things were getting interesting. It wasn't, she told herself, as if she were still sixteen.

Of course, she understood now why he had backed away from her when she was sixteen. As a young girl in the agony of her first crush on an adult male, though, she hadn't understood then. Instead, she'd been hurt by his reluctance to spend time with her, once he sensed her response to him. Naturally, without any fuel to keep it burning, the crush had died. Less than two years ago, however, the response had come rushing back so strongly, it couldn't be denied. At Max and Jeanie's wedding, when Rolph had taken her into his arms to dance, she'd felt as

flustered and excited as she had at sixteen—
sensations she'd never really experienced with
anyone but Rolph. Though she'd tried to tell
herself that weddings aroused those kinds of
feelings in people, she'd known deep inside that
what she felt for Rolph was more than wedding-
induced sentiment. The way he danced with her
that night, she'd thought maybe he felt it too.

That hope, along with her mother's ill health,
had helped her decide to move back to Victoria
shortly after the wedding. But, though she'd
been home for over a year, Rolph had shown no
signs that he shared her feelings. He was
friendly enough whenever their families got together, which was often, but he certainly didn't
seem to care for her any differently than Max
did.

Until recently. Until the day he hired her. Yet
each time he touched her, either deliberately or
by accident, he looked as if someone had poked
him with a cattle prod, and ran.

Maybe she should come straight out and tell
him how she felt. She contemplated that for a
moment, then rejected the idea. No, not without
a little more encouragement on his part. If he
really didn't feel that way about her, it would
mean the end of their valued friendship. She'd
already lost that once, because of the way she
acted at sixteen, and she hadn't completely
regained it, even now.

Marian drew her gaze back to her own desk
and the listings waiting there to be categorized.
She would simply have to be patient.

She smiled. But not for long.

Two

Rolph had spent so many hours deliberately not looking at Marian, when he finally did turn his head her way, his neck was stiff. So, he realized, was hers. She'd taken her hair down so it tumbled around her shoulders, and she was rubbing the back of her neck as if it hurt.

"You've sat there too long," he said, standing and walking up behind her. He pushed her hand and hair away, then massaged her neck. Her muscles were tight, and he kneaded them with his thumbs. Lord her skin was silky! he couldn't help thinking. He shouldn't do this, but hell, he'd given her massages before. *Yeah*, said a voice inside him. *When she was a skinny twelve-year-old killing herself to make the swim team.* She wasn't skinny anymore, and she wasn't twelve, and a lot of things had changed. Hell, she hadn't been skinny for a long time. Briefly, the memory of her sixteen-year-old body pressed against his flashed through his mind, and he cringed with shame. But for all that, he couldn't stop touching her. This was . . . different.

Marian nearly groaned aloud at the sensations his touch aroused in her. While his thumbs worked on the taut muscles in her neck and shoulders, his fingers circled over her collarbone, doing incredible things to other parts of her anatomy far removed from the places he touched. She tried to breathe. It was nearly impossible, but she managed to suck in enough air to speak.

"You said earlier that you had trouble keeping women interested," she said faintly. "If you gave them all a massage like this, you'd never get rid of them. You'd have them stacked up in your closets."

"You think so?" He didn't sound convinced. He spread his hands wide and worked farther down her back. She wished she wasn't wearing a blouse. She wished she wasn't wearing anything.

She sighed. "Why do *you* think they don't stay interested for very long?"

"Oh, sometimes they do," he said. "I was exaggerating when I said that. But it's finding a woman willing to make a commitment that I'm having trouble with. Those who are willing, aren't the kind I want. The kind that interest me are never willing to commit."

"What . . . kind of commitment?" Dammit, her voice was too squeaky!

"The usual kind. You know, marriage, home, family."

"Oh. You want that?" Lordy, she thought. Now her voice was too husky, throaty, all but purring.

"Of course I want marriage." He sounded surprised that she would ask. "I'm thirty-six years old, Marian. It's time I settled down. Not that I expect you to understand that, not with your personality, your life-style, but it's what I want. A wife, babies, a picket fence covered with roses, and all that. I wouldn't insist on the family right away, of course. I like the idea of a couple being a couple for a year or two or three before the babies come along. Time to travel, time to take life easy, time to drift a bit."

She twisted her head around and looked at him from under a fan of hair. "Really? I thought you considered drifting a waste of time. I thought you were married to your business."

"Maybe I am, but that would change the minute I found the right lady."

She swallowed hard. "I see. And are you actively searching?"

He paused, looking off into the distance. "Probably not. Not yet, at any rate. Ideally, I'll have someone fully trained to leave in charge here for a few months, then I'll find my permanent lady, get married, and take a nice long honeymoon, sail *Sunrise* up to Alaska, or maybe down to Mexico, even through the Canal and into the Caribbean."

"Sounds heavenly," she murmured, and dropped her head down to her desk, resting her brow on her folded arms and letting herself relax into his massage as dreams swirled and collided in her mind. She and Rolph, a house, a picket fence, babies and roses and other sweet, growing things. But first, the ocean, the solitude, each other, drifting, sharing *Sunrise*.

"Don't kid yourself." His voice broke into her beautiful dream. "You'd hate it."

"Why do you say that? I love sailing."

"The sailing part, sure, but it's what comes after the honeymoon that you'd hate, and don't try to deny it." His laugh sounded strained. "You're a tumbleweed at heart, Marian. We both know it."

"Not—" Not any longer, she was going to say, but his hands curved around her back, warm through the fabric of her blouse, thumbs sliding downward along her spine, fingertips dangerously close to the sensitive sides of her breasts. Air escaped her in a long sigh, and she lifted her head, letting her hair fall down over her back.

With an impatient gesture, he gathered her hair and twisted it into a rope, flipping it forward out of his way. Then he astounded her, thrilled her, by stroking his hand slowly, sensuously, down over the twist of hair as it lay across her shoulder and chest.

"Your hair—" She heard him swallow, then he jerked both of his hands back. "It feels like satin," he said. "And it smells . . . good." For just an instant, he touched it again as if he couldn't help himself.

She was melting inside as she half turned, gazing up at him. "Does it?"

He licked his lips. With one large, warm hand under her chin, he tilted her head back and stared down at her. His eyes were luminous and filled with desire—as well as confusion and doubt. "Yes," he said softly. "It does."

"Rolph . . ." Her voice was little more than a whisper. She lifted a hand and touched his face, curling her fingers around his jaw.

He shuddered. "I—I think you'd better go home now, Marian. It's late."

She dropped her hand. "All right," she whispered, and smiled at him. Her heart stopped as his thumb traced the smile.

"When did you get so beautiful?" he asked huskily, surprising her yet again.

"I . . . don't know. I didn't know I was." Men had told her she was, but she'd never really believed it. "Beautiful" was just what a man on the hunt said when he wanted a woman to succumb to his charm. Yet when Rolph looked at her that way, when he said it, she believed him. She moistened her lips; they tingled from his touch.

"You are," he said. "Take it from an old connoisseur of women, you are very, very beautiful." His hand slid down her throat an inch or two. One finger stroked the skin just below her left ear. "And your skin is incredibly soft." His thumb grazed the hammering pulse in her throat, hesitated, then returned and rested lightly. Her head grew light as her breath caught. He was going to kiss her. And if he didn't, she was going to faint from wanting it.

Again, she lifted her hand, this time wrapping her fingers around his wrist. "Rolph?" She touched his cheek with her other hand as he had touched hers, tentatively, softly, and then slid her fingers to the back of his neck as he bent lower, lower, his breath warm and arousing on her face.

"No," he said, going rigid, his voice ragged. "I can't." But he did, and she welcomed the feel of his lips on hers, parting hers, as he lifted her up out of her chair and wrapped her in his arms. She was weak, dizzy, and delighted as she clung to his shoulders, but then it was over and she was back in her chair, staring up at him as he slowly backed away from her.

It was as if a freight train had run through the room, Marian thought dimly, hearing a rushing sound in her ears, feeling her whole body trembling, her mouth burning.

"I'm sorry," he said. "Oh, hell, Marian! I shouldn't have done that."

"Why not?" she asked in a small voice.

He stared at her for a long, throbbing moment, then unclenched his fists and stepped back another foot, his eyes suddenly cold as ice. Was he angry or disappointed? she wondered. In himself? In her?

"Because we work together," he said. "Because we've been friends too long to screw it all up by succumbing to a moment's . . . lust. And because we have different goals in life."

He turned and strode to the filing cabinet on the other side of the office. "Here," he said, taking two thick folders from a drawer. "The specs on *Windrider* and *Neo Cleo*. Go home and read them. Meet me at berth 18, Seven Oaks Marina, at nine o'clock tomorrow morning, and we'll go over both boats so you can discuss them intelligently with the Mastersons."

Without waiting for her to reply, he walked out of the office and down the hall to the door that led to his private quarters. As he closed the door behind him, she heard the lock snick tight.

When her legs would bear her weight, Marian stood up, gathered her purse and jacket, and nearly ran all the way to her car.

How in the world was she going to convince Rolph McKenzie that not only should he have done what he did, but he should do a whole lot more besides?

She was halfway home, waiting at a red light that seemed destined never to change, when she was struck by an unwelcome thought. *She* was the one being trained to take over so that Rolph and his "committed" lady could take off on an extended honeymoon aboard *Sunrise VII.* That wouldn't do at all! Somehow, her plans and his were going to have to get onto the same track and head in the same direction.

Trouble was, she didn't have the faintest idea how to make it all happen.

"Max, I need to talk to you." Twenty-four hours had passed since Rolph had kissed Marian and he was no calmer about it. In fact, he thought, his feelings were even more confused. Maybe his brother could help him sort it out.

"Sure, Rolph. Phone do, or do you want it personal and face to face?"

Rolph's palms were slick with sweat. He needed answers and he needed them now. "This is fine," he said, then said nothing more, not knowing where to begin.

"You have a problem or something?" Max prompted when the silence became uncomfortable.

"I guess so. It's just a . . . dilemma I find myself in."

"Uh-huh. What's up?"

"It's Marian."

"Not working out? You didn't expect her to, so what's the big deal? If she's screwing up, tell her so and let her go." Max chuckled. "Of course, you'll have to deal with the wrath of Jeanie. And," he added sternly, "you'll have to replace her at once. Remember my investment."

"It's not that. Actually, she's doing a hell of a lot better than I anticipated."

"So?" What's the problem?"

"It's nothing to do with work. It's more on a personal note."

There was silence for several seconds, then Max said carefully, "Yes?"

"She's my responsibility and I'm not protecting her properly."

"You feel responsible for *Marian*?" Max sounded incredulous. "Why the hell should you feel responsible for her?"

"I just feel it's my place to take care of her, and I've been doing a pretty poor job of it."

"Again, why should you? She's no kid, Rolph."

"I know that, but she's a girl . . . a woman." Lord, was she ever! he thought. "Against my better judgment, I brought her to work in the marina. I mean, it would be different if I still had my office at the house, the way you do, but here she's exposed to the kind of men who live or work in a mostly masculine environment, whistling and shouting and treating her like . . ."

"Like what?"

"I don't know. Just all that whistling and shouting. They make comments." In fact, that hadn't happened since the first day, but Rolph knew the men were all *thinking* things. "They try to date her. It's insulting."

"Marian feels insulted because she's being asked on dates? Haven't guys been asking her out since she was too young to shave her legs? Now, all of a sudden she's complaining? That doesn't sound like the Marian Crane we know and love."

"Well, to be honest, she's not complaining. In fact, she's never mentioned it. She just walks on by as they all ogle her, and she doesn't even seem to notice that any one of them would be all over her if she gave him half a chance."

"Then why worry about it? Besides, are they all after her body? I mean, it's not as if she's exclusive in the marina, or her body's the only one to whistle at. It's a nice little body and all that, but it's just another female shape. Nowhere near as good as Jeanie's. Guys whistle at her too. I think she enjoys it. Is that what's got you in a sweat?"

"What, that maybe Marian likes it?" Rolph sat up straight. "Of course not! I told you, she doesn't appear to notice." Was Max crazy? he wondered. Marian's body was far more attractive than Jeanie's. That must be what love did to a guy, blinded him to the very real attractions of other women.

"Then what?" Max asked, interrupting Rolph's thoughts. "Why should you care if they whistle?"

"I told you that too. I'm responsible for her, dammit. You'd feel the same way, if you'd brought her to a place like this. Hell, she's the nearest thing to a little sister we've ever had." And he remembered well the day Max had forcibly reminded him of that very fact.

"A place like what? That's a marina you're running, not a skid road pool hall! Hey, come on, Rolph, loosen up! That was years ago you made yourself responsible for her."

"We both did. Don't tell me you wouldn't feel the same way if someone were threatening her." For Pete's sake, he thought, had Max forgotten the way he'd acted when he'd thought Rolph himself was threatening the sanctity of Marian's virginity? Rolph certainly hadn't, and that only added to his guilt over yesterday's kiss.

"I *am* telling you that," Max said. "I think she can take care of any threats that might come her way. A guy would have to be nuts to take on every man who showed an interest in Marian Crane. It'd be a full-time job."

The silence that followed those words was filled with thoughts that fortunately remained unspoken, until Max said, "Unless . . . Well, unless he was interested in her himself? Was maybe thinking of taking her on as a full-time commitment?"

"What the hell does that mean?" Rolph barked.

"Nothing, nothing at all," Max said quickly. "Look, just relax and go with the flow. I'm pretty sure Marian can deal with whatever the boating community down there dishes out."

"Maybe. But . . . there's this guy who suddenly has the hots for her. A guy who's too old for her. What would you do if you felt responsible for a woman's safety and well-being, and some man started coming on to her and you knew she didn't feel comfortable with it?"

"How do you know she doesn't feel comfortable? Has she said she doesn't like this man?"

"No. I guess she *likes* him okay, but when I . . . when I saw him touch her, she turned deathly white and started shaking, so I know she hated it."

"Well, if you're sure of that, and just as sure that the guy might make another move that she'd hate, I'd take him aside, explain to him that I looked upon her as a sister, and if he touched one hair on her pretty little head without her express permission, I'd break both his kneecaps and anything else I could reach with my sledge-hammer. But if," Max continued, "there was a possibility that she got pale and shaky because she found the guy's touch disturbing for different reasons, then maybe it would be best to let nature take its course."

Rolph said nothing. His mind was whirling frantically, spinning out of control.

"Well?" Max asked after a moment.

"Well, what?"

"You gonna do it?"

"Let nature take its course?" he shouted. "Hell, no!"

"Then, I guess it must be kneecap time," Max replied cheerfully.

Rolph blew out a long breath. Easy for his brother to feel sanguine. He wasn't faced with a complication like this one. What if Marian *had* turned white and shaky for the reasons Max suggested? Her lips had parted so sweetly under his, and maybe it hadn't been from surprise or shock. What if she was as interested in him as he was in her? Why not find out? Why not go for it? The thought, when he dwelled on it for more than three or four seconds, was breathtaking. But it was insane too.

Marian's staying power was about as long as that of a marshmallow on a bonfire. He wanted someone capable of commitment; therefore, he was not interested in her. He couldn't afford to be. So if he was, if his body was, he was simply going to have to curtail it.

"Right," he said. "Kneecap time. You can consider it done."

As Rolph hung up, though, his mind was whirling again, with images of the day's events flipping over and over like a film out of whack. Marian, standing on the deck of *Windrider,* as fresh and as bright as the morning. Marian, bent over, as she poked her nose into *Neo Cleo*'s bilges. Marian smiling at him while he wiped a smear of grease from her face. He could still feel the delicate bones of her cheek and chin as if they were imprinted on his hand.

What was it going to do to him, he wondered, dancing with her that night, now that she had his hormones raging like starving lions? He drew in a deep breath. Would dancing with her be enough?

Oh, hell, he thought, why take the risk? Why not simply call her and cancel? Why not lie and tell her the Mastersons couldn't make it?

With a heavy sigh, he reached for the phone.

"My God," Rolph said, his gaze sweeping over Marian as she stood in the doorway to her apartment. "Is that a dress, or are you still in your underwear?"

"A dress," she said sunnily, clasping her hands high above her head and turning in a circle. "Like it?" She smiled as if she knew he did, and let her arms fall to her sides. "Come on in. Can I get you a drink before we go?"

"No," he said, his voice sounding strangled. "We're meeting the Mastersons at their hotel in less than half an hour."

A dress, he thought. She was planning to go out with him wearing that dress? She was planning to sit across a table from him and eat dinner, wearing that dress? She was planning to dance with him, for heaven's sake! The damn dress was a lime green concoction and had three tiers of fluffy gathered stuff that formed a very short, extremely flirtatious skirt. As for the top, he's seen swimsuits that were less scanty.

He swallowed against the sudden dryness in his throat and forcibly reminded himself of what Max had said about sledge-hammers and kneecaps, and, what Marian herself had said about her former husband. *I was twenty. He was twenty-eight. We were worlds apart . . .* Worlds apart and eight years, he mused. That was exactly the age difference between himself and Marian. In the normal course of events, eight years was nothing. But this was Marian. She was special. And he wouldn't have just Max to deal with if he put one finger on her against her will, but his parents and hers and his own guilty conscience.

But yes, dammit, he liked her dress. He liked it far too well. "I . . . uh . . . Well, that dress is sort of revealing, isn't it?"

"Would you say that if your date was wearing it, or are you only saying it because your assistant's wearing it?" she asked pertly, the tilt of her chin showing a certain disdain.

As well it should, he thought. And she was right to remind him of their working relationship, as he'd reminded her the day before. If he'd thought for a few minutes then that she might be interested in him as a man, he'd been wrong. He couldn't permit himself to think of her as a woman, either. He never had before, not until recently. Why couldn't he control his feelings better than this? He didn't want to see her as a woman, only . . . she looked like a woman, and smelled like a woman and, when she smiled, he reacted just like a man.

All because that damned dress looked like a slip.

He really should have followed through with his intention to cancel.

"Don't you . . . uh, don't you have something to put over it?" he asked.

"Of course," she said, and picked up a soft, sheer white thing that felt, as she handed it to him, about as substantial as cobwebs. He draped it around her shoulders, his gaze lingering on her smooth, creamy skin. For just an instant, he let himself touch her. She smiled at him over her shoulder, and he quickly dropped his hands, trying not to breathe too deeply. The scent of her perfume did things to his libido that had no business happening.

She scooped up a white evening purse and preceded him out of her apartment. As he followed, he noticed how she'd swept her hair up to the back of her head, securing it, he guessed, with many hairpins. It gleamed like polished gold, tempting him to pull out every one of those pins and let it cascade down her back. He clenched his teeth and followed her down the stairs. Her slim waist looked even smaller in the form-fitting dress, just the right size for his hands to encircle. Her sweetly rounded hips swayed as she walked. Her long, beautiful legs were smooth and he knew they'd feel like satin to the touch, as would that deep vee of bare skin revealed by the open back of her dress. For the sake of his own sanity, he would not, absolutely would not, dance with her that night.

Rolph swung Marian aside to let another couple pass on the dance floor, and the motion brought her soft breasts against his chest. She wasn't wearing a bra. He'd known that, of course. The back of her dress, cut low the way it was, made the wearing of one impossible. He drew in a deep breath and set her back several inches. That, unfortunately, had the effect of letting her thighs brush his.

"Mmm, you've always been a wonderful dancer," she said. "Remember when you taught me how to slow dance?"

He'd been thinking about that since they'd walked onto the dance floor. He'd been thinking of that while he massaged her neck the day before. He'd been thinking of that when Max started talking about sledge-hammers and kneecaps. More than ten years ago, Max had walked in on that dance lesson and caught Rolph holding Marian too tightly, completely enraptured, caught up in the sensuality of the dance and the girl. He had fully forgotten that the woman in his arms, all quivery and starry-eyed and soft in response to his undeniable hardness, was Marian, and that she was no woman, but a sixteen-year-old girl. Forbidden territory.

Rolph winced, remembering the verbal pounding he'd taken from his brother, and the overwhelming guilt that for years had kept him from repeating that utterly stupid action. But what he'd felt all those years ago didn't come close to what he was suffering now.

"No, I don't remember," he said brusquely.

After a confused glance into his eyes, Marian lowered her head.

"Okay, okay, I remember," he said, gently stroking her back by way of apology. "It seems so long ago, though, it makes me feel old thinking about it."

Damn! he thought. How could he have let himself be goaded into dancing with her just by watching Slim Masterson do that very thing?

Slim was old enough to be Marian's father and clearly was in love with his wife of thirty-some years, yet a wave of intense jealousy had washed over Rolph when he saw Slim's broad hand planted squarely in the center of Marian's bare back. There was, of course, no other place for him to put his hand while waltzing, except maybe on her hip, so Slim had had no choice. Neither did Rolph. But the feel of her warm skin and supple muscles threatened his equilibrium.

He had to get off the floor. He strained to see if their main course was by any chance being delivered to their table, but knew it would not be as long as they and their guests were dancing.

"Looking for someone?" Marian asked.

Her smile stilled his breath in his chest. Every time she smiled at him like that, he felt as if he were in free-fall. Now that he knew the feel of her lips, the taste of them, he craved them again. Her eyes were so big and deep, he wanted to drift away in them. Her voice, humming the tune the band was playing, vibrated in his blood. Oh, hell, what was he going to do?

"Rolph?"

"I'm wondering about dinner," he said. "We old folks need sustenance."

"You?" She blinked at him, then grinned. "Would you cut that out? That's the second time you've made a remark like that. You're not old."

"Compared to you I am," he said, and let go of her hand for an instant to tug at the knot of his tie.

With her hand free, she stole the opportunity to place it on his shoulder and link it with its mate behind his neck. Leaning back from him, she brought their hips into alignment and let their thighs touch again. She smiled up at him, innocent and carefree.

"For goodness sake!" she said, "I'm twenty-eight and you're thirty-six. That, my friend, makes us contemporaries."

"Yes, all right, but I find it hard to remember that," he said. "I tend to think of you as just barely out of your teens."

Her subtle movement against him snatched the breath from his lungs. "I'll just have to find ways to remind you, then, won't I?" she murmured.

He stared at her. Had she meant to move like that? She did it again. He swallowed a pained gasp. "Are you trying to flirt with me, Marian?"

She laughed. "Now, really, Rolph, why would I do a thing like that?"

"How do I know? How does anybody ever know why you might do anything? You're a law unto yourself, a free spirit, a butterfly touching the edges of life. I don't ask *why* about you anymore."

"Maybe you should," she said, suddenly looking serious and very unlike the laughing girl she'd been only moments before. "And maybe you should try flirting back. Didn't you say you wanted to learn how to get along with women?"

At that point, the band members played a fanfare to signal the end of the set and laid their instruments aside. Marian led the way off the floor and Rolph followed, telling himself it was ridiculous to feel disappointed that she'd only been offering him a lesson in casual flirtation. He wasn't looking for anything else. Not from her.

Three

"That," said Slim Masterson, leaning back in his chair, "was one of the best meals I've had in a long time."

"Amen," his wife Ethel said, dabbing at her lips with a pink linen napkin. As a server whisked away their plates while another brought the coffee and brandy Rolph had ordered, she sat forward eagerly. "Now can we talk about boats?"

"That's my girl," Slim said, shaking his head. "If she'd had her way, we'd have spent the evening on our hands and knees inspecting decks, rigging, and electronics, instead of enjoying this place and pleasant company."

Ethel patted his hand indulgently. "Somebody has to take care of business." She glanced between Marian and Rolph, then fixed her sharp gaze on Marian. "Well? Are we going to sit and sip brandy like these two, or are we going to start talking turkey?"

Marian smiled. "Gobble, gobble, gobble," she

said, and reached under the table to pull out Rolph's briefcase. "May I?" she asked him.

With a smile in his eyes, he nodded.

"Starting with *Windrider*," she said, as she opened the briefcase, "we have a fifty-foot cutter, John Alden design, built in 1965 by Cooper-Westhall. She's fiberglass, built to Lloyds' specs, and is ideal for charter work in that she sleeps ten comfortably."

She went on to discuss *Windrider*'s excellent long-range fuel and freshwater capacity, and her electronics. When she finished, she handed each of the clients a sheaf of papers. "You can go over these at your leisure before we see the boat in the morning. From what Rolph tells me, *Windrider* is more the boat for you than *Neo Cleo*, though with her width and extra three feet in length, *Cleo* has more below-decks space."

"That's right," Rolph said. "And she's a ketch, while *Windrider*'s a cutter. I know you've expressed interest in a three-master, but there aren't many of those on the market just now, as I'm sure you've discovered. But either one of these will make you a fine charter boat."

The conversation swung into a spirited discussion of the relative merits of the two boats Sunrise Brokerage was offering, as well as others the Mastersons had seen in a buying tour that had taken them from Scandinavia to Hawaii and many points between.

"Of course, what we really want, we can't have," Ethel said wistfully.

Rolph tilted his head questioningly. "What is that?"

"The schooner *Catriona*," Slim replied. "We spent our honeymoon aboard her on a three-month cruise around the Great Barrier Reef thirty-six years ago. We fell in love with her, and with the life. That was when we decided that on retirement, we'd buy *Catriona* and go into the charter business ourselves. Living in Barbados, we have the ideal base for such an operation."

Ethel propped her elbows on the table, her eyes bright as if she were seeing the ship of her dreams. "She was sixty feet overall, schooner-rigged, Burmese teak decks, slept a dozen in comfort, and handled like a real lady with a minimum of crew." Her expression became indignant. "We heard ten or twelve years back that she'd been sold, renamed *Felicity*, and was being used to haul freight in the Seychelles."

Marian could see the older woman took that as a personal affront. "It's sad when things like that happen to beautiful ships."

"And she was a beauty," Slim said. "The workmanship that went into her construction was superb. She was built in Glasgow in the fifties, a wooden boat, of course, but built to last. The detailing was exquisite. Why, there was a compass rose three feet across carved into the walnut headboard of the berth in the captain's cabin, and a smaller one in each of the others. Every porthole had a hand-carved rim of the finest walrus ivory, and each berth was gimballed to reduce sway in heavy seas."

Compass roses? Ivory porthole rims? Marian repeated silently, feeling goose bumps rise on her arms. She rubbed them quickly and opened her mouth to speak, then hesitated, listening while Slim and Ethel went on talking about the beautiful *Catriona*.

"Do you know where she is now?" she asked

moments later, when she had her excitement under control.

Slim shrugged. "We have no idea. She disappeared from the Seychelles several years ago and we haven't been able to trace her. She must have gone down somewhere. A boat like that wouldn't just disappear. If she were still under sail, someone would know where she was. If we could find her, no matter what her condition, we'd buy her, partly out of sentiment, but mostly because we believe in her and know she's the right ship for us."

Ethel sighed. "Of course, we'll settle for something else, but there will never be another ship like *Catriona*."

"Never mind." Slim stood and took his wife's hand, pulling her to her feet. "Let's not waste that great band. Come and dance a bit before we go back to the hotel."

"Rolph!" Marian said excitedly when their clients were out of hearing range. "I know where *Catriona* is! But if we tell them, they'll be able to buy her for a song and we'll be out a sale. What should I do?"

He cocked an eyebrow, obviously not really believing her. "Take it easy. What makes you so sure you know where *Catriona* is? Honey, they've been searching for the right boat, and I assume that means her, for over a year. If they couldn't find her, either as *Catriona* or *Felicity*, what makes you think you can?"

She gripped his hand in both of hers. "Because I know where she is, I tell you. Her present name is *Portside Queen* and she's tied up to a dock in a little tourist town outside Adelaide, Australia. She's used as a gift shop and museum. I know that because I worked aboard her for two months while looking for a crew berth on a boat headed back this way. That was four or five years ago, but what if she's still there?"

"If she's called *Portside Queen,* how do you know she's the right one?"

"Because of the carved compass roses. Rolph, believe me, she's the one! And the Mastersons want her."

"Sweetheart, that was sentiment talking. She's a wooden boat. If she's been sitting tied up to a dock for heaven knows how many years, she's probably rotten right through."

"No, I don't think so. Sandy, the man who owns her, hauls her out every year and has her scraped and painted. He doesn't want his museum sinking under him, you know."

"Maybe he doesn't want his museum sold out from under him, either. Assuming he still owns her. You did say it was four or five years ago you last saw her."

"But we could try. What would it hurt to go have a look? Rolph, she must have been a beauty in her day. Very beamy, with pure, graceful lines. I used to think what a shame it was to see her so trapped, growing shabbier and shabbier. But I could tell that she'd been built to last, just like Slim said. She was a strong ship, a sound one, and I'd stand on her bows picturing her under full sail, set free to fly. Maybe she still could. Listen, why don't we buy her, do a refit, and then sell her to the Mastersons? You heard Slim. He said they'd buy her no matter what. And Rolph, think what a coup finding her would be for the business!"

He laughed at her, then tapped her nose with his finger. "I'm thinking, but you're not. I agree it's worth a try. It's worth investigating. But we don't buy her and do the refit, then tell the Mastersons. Use your head, Marian. We don't own either of the boats we've been offering to them tonight, do we?"

She shook her head. "No. Of course not. You're right. I wasn't thinking. We'll get a finder's fee, though. I'll—"

She was interrupted by the Mastersons' return to the table. "We're going to head back to our hotel now, old boy," Slim said, his arm around Ethel's waist. "You intend to pick us up there in the morning, I understand?"

"That's right," Rolph said. "But would you mind sitting down again, both of you? There's something you need to know. Marian thinks she might have a line on *Catriona*."

The Mastersons both sat, abruptly, their faces expressing combined disbelief and hope.

"You do? But how? Where?"

Marian explained briefly.

"Call him," Ethel said decisively. "Can we get a phone to the table?"

"There's a courtesy office in the back", Rolph said, signaling for a waiter. "I'm sure we can be accommodated there."

The manager of the club unlocked the office for them, and Rolph seated Marian at the large oak desk. "Go for it," he murmured as he slid the phone closer to her.

"Yes," Slim said. "Get *Catriona* for us, my dear, and you'll have earned yourself a healthy commission."

"Not me," she said. "That belongs to Sunrise Brokerage."

"The finder's fee does," Rolph said, touching the back of her neck with his fingers. "But the standard commission is all yours."

When the connection was made, and Marian had identified herself and apologized for calling in the middle of the night, the sleepy, astounded Australian said that yes, his boat had once been named *Catriona*. It was in decent shape, he added, and he would consider selling if the price were right. A deal was struck in principle in just a few minutes. Pending the outcome of a marine surveyor's report and a personal inspection by the Mastersons, *Portside Queen*, formerly *Felicity* and *Catriona*, would change hands. Hopefully for the last time.

Beaming, Slim spun his wife around and kissed her soundly, then did the same to Marian while Rolph, offering his hand to Ethel, was swept into an exuberant hug.

"We did it! We did it!" Ethel exclaimed. "Or Marian did! Fantastic, wonderful, incredible girl! You're a miracle-worker!" She hugged Marian tightly while Rolph and Slim pounded each other on the back. Then, as Slim reached for his wife again, Marian hugged Rolph tightly.

"Thank you, thank you!" she said.

His arms loosely around her, he looked bemused. "Thank *me*? What for?"

"For this wonderful job! Oh, I love making people happy, Rolph! If I didn't work for you, this never would have happened." Impulsively, she wrapped her hands around his neck, pulled his head down, and kissed him on the mouth.

Again, at the touch of his lips on hers, Marian felt faint and dizzy, as if something solid had shifted underfoot. The feel of his mouth, hard and hot on hers, set up such a reaction in her, she didn't think she could stand it. But she couldn't bear for it to stop, either. His arms tightened around her, and he hauled her fully against him, letting her feel every solid, muscular ridge of his body. She loved it and wanted more, more, more . . . and could have wept in frustration when a laughing Slim tapped Rolph on the shoulder.

"Hey, hey! Break it up. We have some serious celebrating to do here, people."

Back at their table, Slim continued effusively, "We'll dance until dawn, drink champagne, and dream of the day *Catriona* sails again. You, my dear Marian, are going to be one of our first guests."

"Thank you," she said. "I can't wait! What a life you two are going to have." A dreamy expression flooded her eyes. "'Faraway places . . .'" she half-sang.

"'Calling me . . .'" Ethel chimed in.

While the women eagerly discussed interesting places, Slim nudged Rolph with an elbow. "You'll be one of our first guests, too, of course," he said, and winked. "A honeymoon trip, maybe, like Ethel and I had? The way that clinch was going, I don't suppose it'll be long. I tell you, boy, there's nothing better than making love in a gimballed berth."

Rolph closed his eyes briefly. "No," he said. "I'm afraid that's not in the cards." *Faraway places . . .* He looked at Marian. She still had that dreamy smile on her face. "But you might offer Marian a job as crew. By the time your refit's finished, her time with me will be over. She'll be ready to move on."

Ethel interrupted the men's quiet conversation. "Didn't you say something about dancing until dawn?"

Slim laughed and stood, taking his wife's

hand. "Come on, you two. You can't let the old folks dance you under the table, can you?"

Marian grinned cheekily. "Never," she said. "Rolph? We don't want to disappoint our guests, do we?"

He hesitated, thinking of the way it had felt to hold her in his arms. Could he stand even ten more minutes of it? He wondered, too, if he could stand to meet Marian's entreating gaze for another ten seconds without giving in. It wasn't the Mastersons he hated to disappoint. He slid one hand up her arm to her shoulder, his palm tingling as it stroked over her smooth skin. "Come on, then," he said gruffly. "If I must, I must."

"Poor Rolph," she said sympathetically. "The sacrifices you make in the name of business."

"It really is criminal. Should be checked into." He smiled down at her, then couldn't look away.

"Absolutely," Marian agreed. Her breath caught in her throat as her gaze locked with his, and her heart beat high and hard and irregularly. She and he were momentarily encapsulated, isolated from the music, from the crowd, from everything but that silent, aching communion between them. So immersed was she in Rolph's eyes, she literally jumped when someone touched her arm.

She whirled, bewildered by the intrusion, finding it almost impossible to form a coherent thought.

"Marian?" The dark-haired man who had touched her seemed taken aback by her reaction. "So sorry. I didn't mean to frighten you. It is Marian Crane, isn't it?" He had a crisp British accent, but it was not regional enough for her to place.

"Yes. Of course." She bit her lip. Who was he?

He looked familiar, but she couldn't recall from when or where.

"You remember me, don't you?" he asked with a smile. "Robin Ames. We met in Hong Kong a few years back. I was married to Adrienne then." His smile never changed. "But I'm not now. Say, I don't suppose your brother would mind if I danced with you, would he?"

"My brother?" Marian's gaze flew to Rolph's set face. "This is Rolph McKenzie. We're not related."

"Oh! Not your brother? I say, forgive me. I wouldn't have intruded if I'd thought . . . But you do look so very much alike, you know." He smiled at both of them. "That blond hair and those green eyes. Even your faces are the same triangular shape. Sorry," he said again. "My mistake."

"Not at all," Marian said. "How nice to see you again, Robin." Actually, it wasn't. Even when married to Adrienne, Robin Ames had tried to put the make on any woman around, but she preferred to be civil. "Rolph is my employer. If you're in the market for a boat of any kind, or have one to sell, Rolph's the man to see."

The two men shook hands briefly, assessing each other. After a few minutes of stiff conversation, Robin Ames smiled again and lifted one of Marian's hands, kissing the backs of her fingers. "Perhaps, McKenzie," he said, looking up, "you'd have no objection if I asked your employee to dance?"

Rolph stepped back from Marian. "Ms. Crane is capable of speaking for herself and making her own decisions."

Marian made one on the spot. "Thank you,

Robin, but Rolph has already asked me. Perhaps another time. Good evening."

"Wait." Again Robin touched her arm. "I'll be in town for several weeks. May I call you?"

She smiled. "I don't think so. I'm terribly busy just now. Good night, Robin. Nice seeing you again."

"Why did you do that?" Rolph asked as Robin left them. "You didn't have to send him away."

"I didn't want to dance with him. I want to dance with you."

Rolph stared down at her, his gaze filled with questions and the same doubts she'd seen the day before when he massaged her neck. "Why?" he asked softly.

She smiled. "Because," she said, deciding she was not yet ready to risk the truth, "you happen to be a far better dancer than Robin Ames." She tucked her arm through his. "You're a better dancer than any man I know. Now, are we going to stand here and discuss it, or are we going to go out there and boogie?"

Rolph capitulated. "Boogie," he said with a laugh. "Let's go."

Capitulation had its rewards, Rolph mused a minute later. That smile of hers! It heated him from the inside out. With a sigh, he succumbed to the intense delight that washed over him as he drew her into his arms. "Heaven help me," he murmured. "I'm going down for the third time."

She twined her arms around his neck, and he rested his cheek atop her head. He would hold her like this for just a moment more, or a month, or maybe, unless she told him to stop, a lifetime. Since she said nothing, just snuggled closer, he wallowed in the sensual world he'd entered, wondering if she felt it too. She had to be. It was too potent to be the product of one set of hormones, too tempting to be refused.

His fingers met at the slight depression of her spine, and he couldn't prevent their exploring that shallow trail all the way up to the nape of her neck, then all the way back down to where her dress stopped them, then all the way back up. . . .

As he slid his hand to her nape again, then around to stroke the skin behind her ear, she tilted her head back and smiled at him, a slow, exquisite smile that took up residence inside his heart, making it glow.

It was heaven. If she died now, Marian thought, she'd die happy. She'd thought the same thing at Max and Jeanie's wedding when she'd danced with Rolph.

Of course, that had been a particularly romantic wedding, with the muted colored lights and decorations, the scent of the Christmas tree, the sweet, flowing music from Sharon Leslie's harp, and the softly spoken vows exchanged by Jeanie and Max.

For the first time, hearing another couple's wedding vows had choked her up with tender emotions. Tears had welled in her eyes. She had blinked hard, but with little effect. They had spilled over, and Rolph had seen them. From his position beside his brother, he had grinned wickedly at her and winked. Later, he'd teased her about it with the affection permitted a long-time friend.

"What were you crying about?" he'd asked.

"Thinking about Jeanie's lost freedom, I suppose?"

She'd shrugged, still not sure in her own mind exactly why she'd found the ceremony so poignant. Ordinarily, since the fiasco of her own marriage, weddings had been something to be avoided. When they could not be, she had often found herself thinking bitter thoughts as the promises were made. Only this wedding had been different.

"Could be that, I guess," she'd said.

When it had come time to catch the bridal bouquet, she'd seen it heading her way and in that instant, caught Rolph's mocking, laughing gaze. She'd ducked, letting Jeanie's flowers sail on by, right into the hands of Sharon, Jeanie's sister.

Less than a year later, Sharon had married that gorgeous French Canadian, Jean-Marc Duval, just as tradition dictated, and Marian had to wonder what would have happened if she hadn't ducked.

But here she was, in Rolph's arms again, feeling distinctly romantic and without a wedding to blame. Nestling close, she rested her head against his chest and gave herself up to the beauty of the moment. His hair was crisp and wavy under her fingers. The skin at his nape was soft and faintly moist. She lifted her face and pressed her lips to his throat, impulsively parting them to sample the salty flavor of his skin. His arms tightened, his body hardened, and she heard him draw in a harsh breath. For just a moment, she thought he might push her away, he relaxed and slid his hand up into her hair. She felt a pin give way, felt it slither down her back, then shivered as his fingers delved deeper into her hair and another pin went flying. Lifting her head, she gazed at him, wanting to speak but finding no words available. She could only convey what she felt by the movements of her body and the expression in her eyes. The moment was over, though, almost as it began. The music stopped, and the Mastersons smiled at them on their way back to the table.

"We'd better go see to our guests," Rolph said, and she heard the reluctance in his voice.

"And then we'll have one more dance?" she asked.

He hesitated. "Okay. One more dance."

The Mastersons had ordered a taxi to take them back to their hotel, and after good nights were said, Rolph and Marian returned to the dance floor.

The crowd had thinned, and "one more dance" turned into several, until Marian lost count. Between sets, they wandered back to their table, talking softly, or simply sitting and saying nothing, just looking at each other or around the room. Always, when the music started again, there was no question that they would dance, and dance, and dance. . . .

A long time later as they swayed together in a corner of the room near the stage, Marian was surprised to see that the band was gone.

"Where's the music coming from?" she asked.

"Tapes," he said. "It's late. We should leave." The heaviness in his voice and his lingering touch on her cheek told her he didn't want the night to end any more than she did.

As she stared up at him, she felt his arms tighten, felt his heat rise. He moistened his lips. She moistened hers. He bent his head. She lifted her face, and his lips covered hers, hard and warm again, firmly commanding as he opened her mouth and touched the inner sides of her lips with his tongue. She shuddered and made a small, pleading sound, and he deepened his caress.

When he lifted his head she was breathless. "Rolph . . ."

"Don't," he murmured. "Lord, don't."

"Don't what?"

"Look at me like that, as if you're going to melt."

"That's how I feel," she said, and held her breath. "Something wonderful happens when we kiss."

His eyes sparkled like green glass, his gaze fixed on her mouth. She could feel it like a caress. It was almost as good as a kiss. Almost. She saw his throat work as he swallowed. "No." His voice was hoarse. "Honey, it's the music, the atmosphere, the dancing. Anyone would do. It's the same as your kissing Slim in the excitement over *Catriona*."

"Rolph . . ." She moved in closer, slipping one hand behind his neck and filtering her fingers through his thick hair. "Do you really believe that?"

He drew in a deep, unsteady breath. "Baby, I'm trying desperately to believe that."

"Why?"

Her soft question stopped Rolph in his tracks. He thought he knew the answer, but looking at her, he found the substance of it slipping away. Her eyes were deep, fathomless pools. Tendrils of her golden hair framed her face, because he'd toyed with it once too often, flicked too many pins onto the floor. One thin strap of her dress hung down over her shoulders. Her scent enfolded him like the heady haze of desire that was rapidly becoming rampant need. That need would be obvious to her if he couldn't find a way to move away from her. But her lips were full and tempting, moist and ready. Her eyes were wide and expectant. Her breasts pressed against his chest as she breathed. Why not? he asked himself. Why not taste her again and see if the magic had simply been a fluke? Why not accept what she offered so sweetly? Why—

"Why?" she asked again, her breath warm and sweet and tinged with wine as it fanned across his face.

He suppressed a groan as he struggled to resist. Across the room, he saw the Englishman, Robin Ames, heading toward the exit door. Robin, a man she'd met in Hong Kong. How many men would come tapping her on the shoulder over the years, reminding her of times past, of places visited? *Faraway places* . . . A life he couldn't offer her. Firmly, he set her back from him, holding her shoulders so she couldn't return.

"Because you've had too much wine," he said, finally answering her. "We both have. It would be wrong. And I like you. I respect you. We work together. And I'm older than you are, more experienced. I know what . . . ambience can do to create a mood, elicit feelings. And I know how false those feelings can be."

As false as the color of the eyes he was staring into, he thought. As false as the shade of the soft hair he couldn't resist touching. He made himself notice those things, made himself remember, though it was hard. He dropped his arms and stepped back from her.

"What makes you so sure those feelings are false?" she asked.

He didn't know, he just knew they had to be. False and transient. As transient as everything else in her life.

"I want reality," he said. "Stability."

Hurt welled up inside Marian, but she'd had years of practice hiding things like that. She arched her brows and smiled. "And I'm not real?" She inched closer. "Is that what you're saying?"

"What I'm saying is that you're wasting your time flirting with me, because I have no intention of wasting my time playing your kind of games."

"This is not a game," she said. Then, as she had in the back office, she gently pulled his head down and kissed him until he couldn't breathe, could hardly stand, and found it necessary to hold her tightly to steady himself.

"Enough," he said presently, dragging her arms from around his neck as he gasped for air, for sanity. "Just stop it, Marian."

She looked at him, her eyes large and serious. "Can either of us stop it, Rolph, now that it's been set in motion?"

He didn't answer. He simply took her elbow in one hand and steered her back to their table, where their two chairs were the only ones still standing square on the floor. He wondered who the phony one was—Marian with her frequently recolored hair, tinted contact lenses, and butterfly existence, or himself, with his insistence that what she offered was not what he wanted out of life. Even if her feelings were false; even if they had been engendered by the romantic music, the seductive atmosphere, and the wine;

even if they were as temporary as everything else in her life, if they were directed at him, he wanted them. He wanted them far too much.

For that reason, after he unlocked her apartment door for her, he let her go with a chaste, brotherly kiss on her forehead and an admonition not to forget to go to Southland Marina first thing Monday morning to see those two boats that were coming on the market.

"That's it?" Marian stared at the door after Rolph closed it. She heard him walking down the corridor, heard the door to the stairs open and shut. She knew he was gone.

"*That's* it!" she said again moments later as she stared at her image in the mirror, then glanced at the framed photograph on her dresser. Normally, the photograph resided deep in a drawer, but she'd taken it out to make a comparison. Robin Ames's words echoed in her mind. *That blond hair and those green eyes. Your brother . . .* It hadn't escaped her notice that Rolph's attitude had hardened immediately after he'd seen Robin leaving the club. It bothered him that they looked alike enough to be mistaken for brother and sister. Did he really care so much what strangers thought?

Obviously, he did.

Again, she looked from her reflection to the photograph of Rolph at Max and Jeanie's wedding. Dammit, they did look alike. Why had she never seen it before?

There was no answer to that, but one thing she could ensure was that neither she nor Rolph nor anybody else would ever see such a resemblance again.

With a nod to the mirror, Marian came to a swift decision. Luckily, she was in good with her hairdresser and confident of getting a Saturday appointment if she declared an emergency.

Come Monday, no one would mistake Marian Crane for Rolph McKenzie's little sister.

Four

Rolph lay on his bed wondering why he was there instead of in— He refused to permit the thought to form. His head still buzzed lightly from the champagne, and his mind was not ready for sleep.

Marian's bed. The thought formed in spite of him. Oh, Lord! It was partly Slim Masterson's fault, with his talk about making love in a gimballed berth.

But the idea of making love with Marian, in or out of a shipboard berth, had plagued him all night, and would have even without those words. Those last dances they'd shared had left him tense and restless. The scent of her lingered in his mind, along with the sound of her laughter, the feel of her in his arms. And her lips. Her incredibly soft, pliable, delicious lips . . .

A honeymoon aboard a newly refitted *Catriona.* The idea had possibilities, all right. He groaned and rolled over, burying his face in his pillow.

Dammit, he already had his honeymoon planned. He was going to spend it aboard *Sunrise VII*. And he was going to spend it and the rest of his life with somebody who wouldn't be secretly dreaming of faraway places. He didn't want a woman who, like Marian, like his own mother, would have to wander until she had searched out all those places.

He wanted a home and he wanted a woman in it. He wanted a family. He wanted his children to have two full-time parents. He needed someone he could trust to stay by his side.

But if that was the case, why did he ache so badly for Marian with a need he could no longer deny, and how was he going to make himself stop?

"Yes?" Kaitlin, the receptionist at Sunrise Brokerage, glanced up, then did a double take when Marian set her briefcase on the front office coffee table. "Marian! Wow, do you look different!"

"Thanks." Marian grinned and turned in a slow circle, showing off her new hairstyle. "Like it?"

"I sure do!" Kaitlin continued to gaze at her in amazement. "I thought your eyes were green."

"Nope." Marian blinked her bright blue eyes. "The green came from contact lenses."

"The difference is incredible," Kaitlin said. "I wonder what the boss's reaction will be."

Something fluttered inside Marian. Ever since she'd left her hairdresser's salon at three o'clock Saturday afternoon, she'd been wondering the same thing. Would Rolph like the way she looked? It had been all she could do not to find some reason to come to the marina during the weekend so she could "casually" bump into him. Now, she couldn't wait for him to see her new look. Sister, huh? She'd show him.

"Is he in the office yet?" she asked.

Kaitlin rolled her eyes. "Not last time I looked. He came out of his apartment twenty minutes ago, unshaven and only half-dressed, eyes looking like pickled beets, and barked something I didn't get. When I asked him to repeat it, he told me to never mind and left again, muttering about coffee. Then he disappeared back inside. To make his own coffee, I presume, since he hasn't showed up since. He's in a mood, let me tell you. This was not the morning for you or Andy to be late, and she only got in ten minutes ago."

Marian glanced through the door to where the secretary, Andrea, sat busy at her typewriter, then looked down at her watch. "I'm not late. I've been at work for an hour already. I was over at Southland putting in bids on two properties we have clients interested in." And, she added silently, collecting some heartwarming whistles and compliments. They'd done a lot for her ego and self-confidence, as much as the new hair color and clear contacts, as much as the slim-cut turquoise slacks and matching jacket she wore. Teamed with a bright purple blouse and scarf and equally bright purple pumps, the outfit was an eye-stopper.

"And I gave Andy permission to be late," she went on. "She had to take her baby for his six-months shots this morning. Rolph knew about it."

At that moment, Rolph strode down the corridor that led from his apartment. All the earlier compliments and whistles faded from her mind under the impact of the pure appreciation that shone in his eyes when he saw her.

"Oh." Rolph heard his own voice crack over that single word as his breath left his lungs in a whoosh. Good Lord, what had she done to herself? he wondered, halting abruptly. She was a redhead again. Not the same shade Mother Nature had endowed her with, but a close approximation. And her hair was cut short. It bounced around her head in a wealth of copper-colored curls that caught the light and flung it to the far corners of the room. Marian gazed at him as he entered the outer office and seemed to be . . . waiting. Waiting and looking at him with eyes the color of the summer sky. Those eyes, that hair . . . The combination took his breath away completely. She was enchanting.

Dammit, she looked beautiful. She looked delicious.

And she looked all of sixteen.

"Oh," he said again. "So you're finally here."

Marian smiled. His gruff tone belied the expression in his eyes. He was staring at her exactly as he had when he'd told her not to look at him like she was about to melt—as if in the next twenty seconds, he was going to do exactly that himself.

She feasted her eyes on him. He wore a freshly pressed fawn-colored suit, a light green shirt, and a deeper green tie. He carried a briefcase in one hand and held a sheaf of papers in the other. His eyes may have looked like pickled beets half an hour before, but they were clear and sharp now. He looked terrific. Strong, energetic, masculine, incredibly virile . . . and totally, gratifyingly stunned.

She met his gaze, reveling in the knowledge that he'd noticed her new hairstyle and color, and that he liked both. "Yes, I'm here," she said. Her smile deepened. "Did you forget I was going to Southland?"

Rolph gave his head a quick shake. "No. Of course not." He had forgotten. Looking at her, he figured he was lucky he could remember his shoe size. He'd been waiting for her to show up for over an hour, going crazy waiting, needing to know if what she'd done to him Friday evening had passed like a forty-eight hour virus, and had maybe even vaccinated him against further infections.

It hadn't. He was just as susceptible to her now as he had been Friday night. Maybe more.

He dropped his briefcase onto the coffee table, and shoved the papers in his hand, in the general direction of Kaitlin's desk. They fell to the floor. He didn't appear to notice. Still looking at Marian, he said, "I . . . uh, need, you to take over for the day, okay? I've got to—I'm going— I'm leaving."

"But—" she began as he accidentally grabbed her briefcase from the coffee table and shouldered past her. "Rolph, you've got my—"

He didn't seem to hear. Hurrying out the door like a man pursued by something large and dangerous, he loped down the ramp to the wharf below, and Marian saw that one of the marina crew had *Sunrise VII* already untied, the engine running, stern swinging out into the harbor. As she raced after him, Rolph leaped aboard, brief-case, suit, tie, city shoes, and all, and said something to the kid. The boy jumped back onto the wharf, scratching his head in perplexity, then stood there, staring at the boat as its stern angled away from the dock.

Marian was only peripherally aware of that as she tore down the ramp, her shoulder bag flopping against her hip, his briefcase, heavier than her own, banging her knee. "Rolph," she called. "Dammit, would you wait? I need that stuff you swiped!"

She ran after him, and as he disappeared into the cockpit of his boat, she kicked off her shoes and leaped aboard, landing on the bow just as it swung away from the float and the engine kicked from reverse into forward.

If she had planned it she couldn't have done it better, Marian thought a moment later as she lay, sprawled and unseen, on the curved bow deck, fighting her body's tendency to slide toward the edge. She caught the wire rail in one hand and slipped through the open hatch onto the V-berth below, managing to haul her shoulder bag and Rolph's briefcase in with her. As the bow swung in a tight arc, she flopped sideways banging her head on the bulkhead. Pushing herself erect, she looked out the porthole at the foaming water rushing by only inches from her nose.

Where the heck were they going in such an all-fired hurry?

Rolph McKenzie was going to get picked up by the harbor police for sure, if he didn't slow down. He was booting out of the marina as if he thought she was still running down the ramp calling his name. He was—or thought he was—escaping her.

With a small, delighted laugh, she settled back onto the berth, crossed her ankles, and wiggled her toes. She didn't know where they were going, but wherever it was, she was going without any shoes.

It didn't matter. She was going with Rolph.

Maybe it was time he learned that once she had made up her mind about something, there was no escaping Marian Millicent Crane.

"Oh, Lord," Rolph muttered, shrugging out of his suit jacket and kicking off his shoes. He glanced at the highly varnished mahogany deck and saw a couple of scratches from the hard soles of those shoes. Never mind, he thought. It wouldn't hurt him to do some sanding and varnishing. It was worth it to have gotten away before he made a complete fool of himself. If he'd stayed at the office another minute, he would have swept Marian into his arms, carried her back to his apartment, and ravished her.

Poor Brewster. The kid must be wondering what the hell was going on. Rolph had told him to take *Sunrise* over to the fuel dock and top up her tanks. He'd been doing just that when Rolph had come flying down the walk, bellowing at the kid to forget it, he'd do it himself.

Guiltily, he glanced astern at where the fuel docks were fast disappearing, and even farther astern, almost expecting to see Marian standing on the wharf looking lost and forlorn. He also glanced just as guiltily at the wash creaming away from the hull and throttled back. After taking off his tie, he unbuttoned his shirt and took it off, too, tossing it on top of his jacket.

He wasn't sorry he'd bolted, but he was glad Marian wasn't standing on the dock. He'd hate to have seen her looking sad and abandoned.

But leaving like that had been the only sane thing to do.

He hadn't even been able to stay long enough to tell her what he wanted done that day while he flew down to Seattle. And he didn't dare ask himself what would happen when he came back from having settled arrangements for his booth at next year's boat show in the Kingdome. That wasn't something he was ready to face just yet. Maybe, if he stayed away for a day or two, that forty-eight hour virus would run its course. Ninety-six hour virus? Six hundred and forty-four? Incurable? Hell!

What he wanted to do was sail, as far and as fast as he could, the wind whistling in the rigging, spume hissing by, waves rollicking against the hull, the shore dropping farther behind, and with it, what he was quickly beginning to see as an insurmountable problem: His growing desire to make love to Marian Crane.

What was stopping him from sailing away, he asked himself, letting the wind cleanse him of his insane fantasies? He wasn't expected in Seattle until late afternoon. What was to stop him from sailing down? Nothing. He picked up his shirt and jacket, shook them out, and hung them from a hook on the mast. Peeling off his socks, he rolled them into a ball and stuffed them in a corner of the seat where they wouldn't pick up too much spray. Then, with his suit pants folded neatly and wearing only his underwear, he cut the motor, quickly set the self-furling sails, trimmed them, fastened the sheets, and took his seat at the helm. Leaning back, his bare legs outthrust and crossed at the ankles, he gave the tiller a nudge with an elbow and felt the bow lift to meet the chop rolling in from the Strait of Juan de Fuca.

For today, at least, he was free of Marian and all the incredible things she did to his libido.

Whew! Marian wiped her brow with the back of her hand. In spite of the open hatch and the salty wind blowing in, the cabin was hot. She had to get out of her office clothes. Surely, she could find something to wear stuffed into one of the lockers. Moving carefully so as not to disturb the trim of the boat and alert Rolph that he had a stowaway, she slid off the berth and shrugged out of her jacket. Of course he'd have to know sooner or later that she was aboard. She'd just prefer it to be later, when they were so far from port that he'd think it not worthwhile to turn back and put her ashore. She'd like a day out on the water with him, and she had the perfect excuse—he'd taken off with her briefcase. Didn't she have a right to chase it down?

So what was her reason for not having told him immediately that she was aboard? she asked herself. Shrugging, she rubbed the small lump on her head and decided that if he asked, she would claim she'd been knocked unconscious.

She stripped off her slacks, put them with her jacket on a hanger in the boat's only hanging locker, then grimaced. The locker held nothing useful, unless she wanted to wear a long yellow slicker or a bright orange floater coat. A quick and careful search of the remaining lockers in the bow turned up nothing other than sleeping bags, life jackets, several unidentifiable pieces of machinery, and one unopened case of sardines.

Moving aft toward the galley area, she searched each locker and bin she came upon, but found no clothing. Clearly, Rolph wasn't in the habit of inviting ladies aboard, at least not ladies who conveniently left items of apparel behind. Then, under one seat in the settee, she struck gold.

Rolph's swim trunks made adequate shorts, she discovered, tugging the briefs up over her hips. One of his T-shirts would complete the costume, if only she could find one.

Not in that locker, among the swim fins and masks and snorkels, but surely in the one opposite?

She knelt on the deck and opened the bin under the seat, then frowned as she reached in and withdrew one of the dozens of books neatly stacked inside.

Well! she thought. Maybe his ladies didn't leave their clothing behind, but they certainly left their reading material. She riffled through the stack of romance novels, finding several by her favorite writers. Lord, there were enough books to keep her happy if they were sailing to China! What a treasure trove!

Forgetting all about T-shirts, Marian continued digging through the stack, opening a book here and there at random, then stopping when she saw passages and phrases marked with yellow highlighter.

In one of the contemporary romances, during a conversation between two women about their ideal man, several words were highlighted. *Strong, tough, macho, sensitive, wise, understanding.* In another, a historical romance, she found a scene in which a pirate was introducing the virgin heroine to passion. She was loving it, loving him, even while she pretended that she thought he was foul and beastly. Her thoughts had been highlighted, her reactions and responses to the feel of the man's hard muscles, the scent of his skin, the sound of his rasping breath and his impassioned words, all of which enhanced the woman's excitement.

Intrigued, never having analyzed romances in this manner, Marian continued flipping through the books, stacking them on the deck beside her and on the settee behind her. Many highlighted sections dealt with what different women perceived as necessary attributes in a man, what thrilled them, what turned them off, what they wanted. Some even had penciled-in notes, such as, *This is a paradox!* And, *How is a guy supposed to be both gentle and strong? Sounds like toilet paper.* And, *Being a romantic hero is impossible. These guys are unreal!*

"Rolph?" she whispered finally as she recognized his scrawl. "Oh, Rolph!"

She sat there with a book open on her lap, staring at it, yet not really seeing the words as she tried to make sense of what he must be attempting. Attempting to learn from books what he believed he'd never learn from life? Trying to be a fictional hero, or a blend of all these fictional heroes? If he thought women really wanted men such as these, someone who always knew what to say and what to do, and could do it seven times a night, then no wonder he wasn't happy with his success rate. No wonder he couldn't find the right woman.

If he wanted to *be* someone completely fictional, she mused on, then he probably also wanted to find someone completely fictional, a dream figure, larger than life and twice as beautiful. No! Whatever else he might be, Rolph was not unintelligent. Surely he recognized these characters as wonderful fantasies, the stories as pure, delightful escapism.

But . . . what if he didn't? Oh Lord, what if he didn't know the stories were merely fantasies? What if he thought this was the way it really was between men and women, or that women wanted only what they read in books? What hope did she have of ever becoming his ideal woman with all these glorious heroines to compete with? Dammit, she was real! She was nobody's fantasy!

But, oddly enough, Marian reflected, sitting back on her heels, Rolph was her fantasy. She could see him, aspects of his personality, in every one of the heroes her favorite authors created, and yet he was much, much more besides. He was real, and he was the hero she'd dreamed of for years, the fantasy that had lived in her imagination since she was a girl, even though she hadn't recognized him.

He was the measure to which she'd held all other men, only to watch them fall short.

She wanted to laugh. She wanted to cry. She wanted to crawl out there on deck, curl up in his lap, and convince him he was the most romantic hero she'd ever known. She wanted to tell him that to her, he was both gentle and strong, loving and kind and tough and wise and, in spite of his obvious intelligence, he was in some ways so damned stupid, she'd like to shake him until his ears fell off!

It wasn't Rolph's ears that fell off, but the towering stack of books on the settee. They tumbled to the deck with a resounding thud as the boat heeled far over to port. She was on her knees trying to gather them up again when the galley hatchway slid open and Rolph swung in, landing with his bare toes only inches from the stack on the floor.

He stared at her kneeling there, eyes wide, mouth agape, a book in one hand, another pressed to the front of her purple blouse, guilt spreading over her face.

"Hi," she said. "I, uh, wanted to talk to you."

"What are you doing with those?"

That told her a lot. He didn't ask "What are you doing here?" or "How did you get aboard?" but "What are you doing with those?"

"Putting them away," she said evenly. "I was looking for a T-shirt. I'd hate to ruin a silk blouse kicking around on a sailboat."

He crouched and picked up several books, not meeting her eyes. A bright flush stained his high cheekbones. "You were looking at my books."

"Yes." It pleased her for some obscure reason that he didn't try to pretend they were someone else's books. "I haven't had a chance to read that one yet." She pointed to the last one he had picked up. "May I?"

He put the book in her outstretched hand, then set the stack back into the locker and turned to collect more. Setting her book aside, Marian helped him, then closed the lid on the locker, and pushed the seat cushion back into place.

Rolph got to his feet. He could just stand in the cabin. His blond hair brushed the ceiling. His mouth was a taut line, and the flush had faded from his cheeks. He looked dangerous now, faintly threatening, his eyes glittering with a light that told her passion was about to erupt—in one form or another. It thrilled and excited her, even while something primal in her cringed and curled back, seeking safety.

Marian arose. She felt better standing, though there was no place to run. At that thought, she frowned. This was the first time she'd ever considered she might need, or want, to run from Rolph. She licked her dry lips and opened her mouth to speak, but he forestalled her.

"You'll find a T-shirt over there," he said, gesturing to a starboard locker. Then he lifted himself back out the hatch, leaving it open for light and air.

When she appeared on deck a minute later, one of his T-shirts covering the swim trunks she wore, he sat looking at her for several moments. Finally he said, "I'm waiting."

"What for?"

He squinted against the sun. "For the laugh."

"Laugh?"

"Aren't you going to laugh at me? I mean, how often is it that you find out a guy you know is a closet romance reader?"

At that moment Marian wanted very badly to be a heroine in one of those books, someone who knew what to say, what to do, to help both of them out of this extremely awkward situation. But she wasn't. She was just a real woman, a woman who wished she were at the bottom of the strait, or at least, back on the other side of it; a woman who wished she hadn't embarrassed him this way, made him feel exposed and humiliated.

Holding up the book she'd borrowed, she said, "I didn't see any notations in this one."

He nodded. "I haven't bothered making notations for a long time, or analyzing. I just read them because I like them."

"Okay, then." She slid onto the stern bench beside him, curling her legs up so her knees touched his thigh and her shoulder rested against his bicep. "Share the best parts of this one with me."

"Marian . . ." His voice was heavy.

"What?" She tilted her head back to look at him.

"I wish . . ." His arm shifted, encircling her shoulder.

"Rolph . . ." She gulped, then whispered, "I wish too."

He looked at her. His one hand tightened on her shoulder, while the other one cradled her chin. "Oh, hell," he muttered. "What am I going to do?" Then he bent and took her mouth in a hard, thrusting kiss that held not one hint of gentleness, yet was the kind of kiss she both wanted and needed, a kiss in which she participated wholeheartedly.

She slid her arms around his solid, warm torso, her fingers digging into his muscular back. He made a sound deep in his chest and tilted her head farther back. His mouth lifted from hers and slid down to her throat, and he murmured words she couldn't make out over the sound of blood pounding in her ears. It didn't matter. She didn't need to hear him. She could feel him, feel his straining muscles as he turned her, swung her half around and across his lap.

His legs were bare, and the hair on his thighs prickled her back where her T-shirt hitched up. His skin was warmed by the sun, and by a heat generated deep within. His shoulder against her cheek was hard, rippling as he moved. She stroked the other one, just to feel it, down over his bicep, up to the side of his neck, back around to his nape, then curving down over his collarbone and lower, to the crisp hair on his chest. Her fingers tangled there, stroking, and she discovered a nipple, hard, distended, growing harder at her touch.

He buried his hands in her curls, forcing her head back so he could have her mouth again. Against her closed lids the sun was a hot, red blanket. He tasted incredible, of salt spray and man. Rolph. His lips were purposeful as his tongue probed deeply; his hands clenched in her hair and then relaxed. One slid down her arm and the other encircled her nape while his mouth gentled, softened. The tip of his tongue touched her upper lip, then her lower, then inside. When his hand slipped down her back, then up under the T-shirt to caress her waist, she trembled. Her stomach muscles convulsed as he stroked his palm over them, and she gasped in pleasure when he cupped her breast.

Arching her back, she pressed herself into his hand, her nipple aching for his touch, but he denied her silent demand, pulling his hand out from under the shirt without undoing her bra.

"Rolph, please," she sighed.

He groaned and gripped the back of her head, pressing her cheek to his bare, heaving chest, holding her tight.

Tentatively, she trailed her hand down his

body, then touched the taut muscles of his thigh.

He sucked in a harsh, unsteady breath and captured her hand, pulling it back up to his chest. "No. Stay still. Don't move. Don't say anything. Please."

Five

She didn't, and he didn't. They sat there, holding each other, his trembling hand stroking her back, her shoulder, touching her hair now and then, until their breathing was back under control.

"Oh, God," he muttered, and said nothing more until a piercing ship's whistle split the silence. Setting her back into the corner of the bench, he adjusted the tiller so that *Sunrise* slipped past a nearby freighter's stern unharmed. Marian glanced at his face. He was pale, his mouth a taut line. His gaze slid away from hers.

After the boat had ridden out the freighter's wake, she picked up the book she had dropped and opened it to the first page, pretending to read. It was easier that way. She didn't want to look at Rolph again. She didn't want to see that terrible regret on his face.

He reached over and tousled her hair. "Hey, Marian, I'm sorry."

She looked up. His expression had scarcely changed. "What for?"

"I shouldn't have done that."

She clenched her teeth. What good would it do to tell him that, by her lights, the only wrong he'd committed was in stopping? He didn't want to know that. He was sick with remorse for having kissed her, for having given in to the primitive need they both felt. If she didn't ease the situation for him somehow, he was likely to abandon ship at the first uninhabited island within swimming distance. From somewhere in her depths, she conjured up a cheeky smile and the strength to aim it at him.

"I've read the books, Rolph. I know what happens to stowaways, the kind of punishment meted out by the chief buccaneer. You make a darned good pirate."

He shot her a disgusted look. "That wasn't what I was doing. I didn't mean to 'punish' you. I'm sorry if you felt that I did."

She became instantly serious. "Then what did you mean, Rolph?"

"Nothing, dammit. Not one damned thing! It was a mistake, all right? Just like Friday. I shouldn't have kissed you. I won't kiss you again. Now keep your head down while we come about. I'd better get you home." He glanced at his watch. "I might still make my flight if the tide doesn't turn before we get into the harbor."

Visions of his following the Mastersons to Australia just to get away from her flooded her mind. "Flight?"

"I was going to fly down to Seattle today, but when I—At the last minute, I decided to sail down." He scowled at her as if suddenly realizing there were questions he should have asked earlier, and hadn't. "How did you get aboard, anyway, and why?"

She explained about the briefcases, about her flying leap, and didn't bother with the lie she'd considered using. She didn't even mention that she'd bumped her head.

"And you didn't see fit to tell me," he asked, "when there was still plenty of time for me to set you ashore?"

"No," she said. "I wanted to come, too. It looked like a great day for a sail."

"Sure. That's our girl, our flibbertigibbet Marian." He frowned at her. "What's the matter? Getting tired of the job already? No problem. You can quit anytime. And I just gave you the perfect excuse. Sexual harassment. Isn't that what they call it when the boss forces unwelcome embraces on his female employee?"

She sprang to her feet and stood with one hand on the boom, anger giving her voice the power and strength his kisses had robbed her of. "I'm *not* tired of the job. I have no intention of quitting. And your embrace was not unwelcome. I did not feel sexually harassed. But if you did, then I can only apologize." She felt her throat tighten and swallowed hard before going on.

"Suddenly, Rolph, a day's sail doesn't sound so appealing. So if you're going to turn this bucket around, go ahead and do it. Even if the boss can take the day off to go cruising down Puget Sound, his assistant cannot."

She ducked into the cabin and slid the hatch home, then slammed the half-door.

The boat did not come about.

• • •

"Marian?"

She didn't look up from where she sat at the galley table, pretending to read.

"You could come to Seattle with me. After all, we're more than halfway there. And as my assistant, maybe you should be in on the decisions that I'll have to make today."

What a load of garbage! Rolph thought. Marian would be long gone by the time next year's Seattle boat show took place, so her input was completely unnecessary. He didn't know why he continued to torture himself like this, but he wanted her with him now that she was here, and he didn't have the strength of will to force himself to take her home.

She flicked a glance at him. "Whatever you say. You're the boss. You're the skipper. I'll sail to Seattle with you, but whatever business you need to conduct there, you'll have to do it alone. I'll stay aboard the boat."

His anger flared. "As you pointed out," he said, his voice grating, "I'm the boss. You'll come with me if I say you will, and help me conduct my business."

"Fine," she said, and stuck one bare foot out toward him. "And let everyone think you don't pay me enough to buy shoes? After all, what people think is of paramount importance to you, isn't it?"

He took a step closer, looking dangerous again. "What's that supposed to mean?"

Marian refused to be intimidated, and stood up. "The words are quite plain, aren't they? What other people think is more important to you than what I think, even more important than what you think. Pleasing strangers takes precedence over pleasing yourself."

He jammed a hand through his hair, shoving the thick waves up into peaks. "What strangers? You're not making any sense."

"Robin Ames, for one. Other people at Estevan's Friday night, people who might think because we have—had—the same coloring, that we were related. That's what all this is about, isn't it? That's why you're having such a hard time dealing with what even I, as stupid and juvenile and uninformed as I apparently am, can tell is a genuine, physical attraction."

She reached up with both hands and fluffed out her red hair. She blinked her blue eyes. "Well, do we look alike now, Rolph? Now that I'm no longer a green-eyed blond, but a blue-eyed redhead, exactly what I was originally, do you still think the general public might mistake me for your sister? And if they do, do you care?"

No! The word exploded in his brain. He didn't care, because he had held her, kissed and tasted her, cupped her breast in his hand. It hadn't mattered then what color her hair or eyes were, or if she looked sixteen or thirty-six, or who thought what about them. But it should have, dammit. What he felt for her he had no business feeling. He could screw up his entire life over a woman like her. "Marian—"

She didn't allow him to finish. She didn't even allow him to begin. Stepping close, she glared at him, hands on hips. "I did this for you!" she said, fluffing her hair again. "And for me, and for all those strangers you worry about so damned much! Look at me! Nobody's going to think I'm your sister, so you didn't have to be ashamed of kissing me out there in the cockpit."

Suddenly, he was as angry as she was. She was so unfair! Didn't she know he was trying to protect her as well as himself? Couldn't she understand that? Hell's bells, it was never like this in those damned romance novels. In them, the women knew how to behave. In them, the woman would have called a halt, or the telephone would have rung, or . . . If he hadn't stopped kissing Marian, he would have lost control of himself and made love to her right out there on deck. He'd have scared her out of her mind with the intensity of his desire, perhaps even disgusted her, as her husband had.

"I wasn't ashamed of it for that reason," he said, struggling to keep his voice down. Romantic heroes didn't yell at women. "I don't care what other people think!"

"No? You were holding me, Rolph, kissing me, touching me, and we were both enjoying it, until that freighter blew its whistle and you realized somebody else might become aware of what we were doing. And that made it bad for you. I don't like having you ashamed of kissing me, Rolph. I don't like having you angry with yourself for wanting me. It makes me feel cheap and unworthy."

"Dammit," he shouted, losing it completely. "I'm not ashamed of kissing you! At least, not for any of those reasons. I don't think you're cheap and unworthy."

She shouted right back. "Then what is your problem?"

Oh, hell! Rolph wiped his forehead with the back of his hand. How could he tell her what his problem was when he didn't fully understand it himself? "I want you," he said in a strangled tone.

She looked young and bewildered and hurt, and he hated himself for doing this to her. "I know," she said quietly, then added with a slight movement that could have been a shrug, "I want you too."

Wham! Something slammed into his chest. "Marian!" he exclaimed, and her name came out all in pieces, jerky, as if it had been yanked from him. Hearing her say those words so casually sent fire ripping through his guts. How could she possibly know what she was saying? If she had the faintest inkling, she wouldn't have told him that, not in such an offhand manner, like saying she wanted a hamburger. Clenching his fists so that he wouldn't snatch her in his arms and show her what that phrase really meant, he said, "You can't just come right out and say that to a guy! It's dangerous and foolish and not something a woman says just like that. If she says it at all, she does so in the throes of passion."

"Maybe in the books you read," she said, with another of those little half-shrugs. "But this isn't fiction. I said it because I want you to know. I said it because it's true." Her voice wobbled and her chin quivered. She firmed both quickly. "I do want you. I want to go to bed with you. I want to make love with you. I want to feel all of you naked against all of me." She laid one hand on his chest, fingers splayed, palm hot against his burning skin. He felt a tremor in her hand as she looked straight into his eyes. "I want to know what it's like to have you inside me."

Her words, accompanied by that gentle touch, nearly stopped his breath. He groaned and clenched his fists tighter. "Marian, don't do this!"

"Why not? Like I said, it's true. And it's not as though you're a stranger I met on a bus five minutes ago." She let her hand trail off him, her fingertips tracking down toward the waistband of his shorts, then leaving him. He felt branded. "It's been building in me a long time, Rolph. I wasn't going to tell you, I was just going to show you. I tried to Friday night, only you weren't looking."

"I was . . . looking." His words came slow and hoarse.

"Sure. Looking. Not touching. Not taking."

"God, Marian! I touched, all right, but . . . No, I didn't take. I can't do that, Marian. I— You—" He broke off, shaking his head. He took a halting step back from her, then another, and another, until he was up against the steep stairs leading to the deck.

Marian smiled at him, a small, sad smile that got to him in a way even her bright, sassy, sexy smile never had. Was there any end to the ways this woman could affect him? He almost said to hell with his scruples, to hell with not starting an affair with a completely incompatible woman, to hell with right and wrong. But she lifted a hand and spoke first.

"It's all right, Rolph. We don't need to talk about it now. I just wanted you to know, so you could think about it, think about me. About us. It's not safe, not having someone on watch here among the islands. Do you want me to take the tiller?"

He stared at her. Did he want her to take the *tiller*? Damn, but she had him rattled, and so hard he didn't think she could even walk to get the hell out of that cabin. A glance out a port-hole showed him steep green shores close to port, though. She was right. They were sailing in waters too confined for them to conduct an argument or discussion or a crazy, impossible seduction below decks. Still he stared at her for another few moments, wondering if there were words in his vocabulary to explain to her exactly what she made him feel. There were not. There weren't even words in his vocabulary to explain to himself exactly what he felt, so he turned and went back to the cockpit. He sat at the tiller, keeping a watch all around while trying not to let his gaze wander to Marian's flame-haired figure, visible through the open hatch as she sat at the galley table, turning the pages of a romance novel as if the world weren't going as nuts for her as it was for him.

I will not cry. I will not cry. I will not cry.

Marian repeated the words to herself like a mantra, staring at the pages of the book, forcing herself to turn them at intervals, to give the appearance of reading. But the tears she fought stung and burned until she knew she couldn't defeat them. Crawling into the berth in the bow, she rolled onto her front and hugged a pillow, letting the tears ooze out. They brought no relief from the stinging and burning inside her, though.

She had done it again. She had flung herself at a man, told him how she felt about him, all but begged him for his love, and watched him turn and walk away. She'd expected from Rolph the sensitivity and compassion she hadn't got-ten from her ex-husband, not a blank-eyed, shocked stare, not a slow shaking of his head and those halting, awkward steps away from her. Sure, she had told him to go, told him to think about what she'd said, but she'd seen in his eyes that he'd already done what thinking he needed to do. He didn't require any time to consider her proposition. He'd made up his mind.

Their dances, their closeness, their undeniable physical response to each other Friday night had been what he'd said, a result of ambience and wine—at least on his part. And today? Those kisses out there on deck? That interlude had been real and wonderful, and left her yearning for more. Yet he had pushed her away.

She wasn't aware of falling asleep, or of the anchor chain being let out, but when Rolph touched the back of her leg with his fingertips, she was instantly, totally awake.

She rolled over and sat up. "Are we in Seattle already?"

"No. We aren't going to Seattle."

"Why?"

He touched her cheek with a finger, trailing it from the corner of her eye to the corner of her mouth, then pausing there. "You've been crying."

She blinked. "We're not going to Seattle because I've been crying?"

He smiled slowly, acknowledging her weak joke. His caressing finger skimmed down over her chin to her throat, then followed the loose neck of the T-shirt around to one side. There, he slid all his fingers just inside the shirt, curving his hand over her shoulder. "We aren't going to Seattle because there's something happening between us that we have to deal with before we can go anywhere at all. So we're anchored in a bay on South Pender Island. Why were you crying?"

She wanted to shrug his hand off, but it felt so warm and strong, so sensuously rough and male, she left it there. She thought of making something up about the tears having been tears of anger, but knew there was no point in trying to lie to Rolph. He knew her too well. He could see right into her soul. Especially now, especially after she'd opened her heart to him. So she told him the truth, as painful as it was, but she tried to sound amused, almost indifferent.

"Because I was stupid." She smiled crookedly. "I hate being stupid. It makes me feel . . . well, stupid." She glanced out the porthole rather than look at him, at the compassion in his eyes. What if it turned to pity?

She changed the subject. "South Pender Island is nowhere near Puget Sound. It's even north of Victoria."

His other hand clamped onto her other shoulder, turning her to face him. "My," he said, shaking her slightly. "How perceptive. I should have had you on deck to navigate." He frowned. "What do you mean, you were stupid?"

She drew in a deep breath and shrugged. "As you pointed out, a woman doesn't just up and say something like that to a guy. Not unless she's pretty sure he'd interested in more than a few casual kisses. I said it, and you weren't, and I feel like a fool."

He drew her against his chest, wrapping his arms around her, and rocked her back and forth for several moments. Then he thrust her away, holding her by the upper arms. "Dammit," he said huskily, "you're throwing guilt at me like mud. I didn't say I didn't want you. I said I did. Do."

Tears stung her eyes once more, but she refused to allow them out. Tilting her chin up, she said, "I'm not trying to make you feel guilty. I'm sorry you do. I don't want you to. Yes, I know you said you want me, but still, you walked away."

He squeezed his eyes shut for an instant as his fingers tightened on her arms. "Right now, Marian," he said, opening his eyes, his chin jutting out with a stubborn streak she'd almost forgotten he had, "right now, there is nothing I want more than I want you, just the way you said, naked, together, me inside you, you surrounding me, taking what I want to give you, giving what I want to take." His voice shook with the intensity of his emotions. "I want you so bad I can't think straight. I'm trying to be sensible, though, trying not to make a big mistake that will hurt not only us, but the people we care about, our families, who have been friends for years. What happens if you and I get together for a while and then blow it? It would make their friendship, the joint celebrations we've always enjoyed, awkward, to say the least. What happens if this is as wrong as I fear it is? That's why we have to talk it through, make sure what we both want is right for both of us."

Her throat ached. She needed so badly to believe that he really did want her, she didn't think she could stand any more of this analysis he seemed so intent on. She wanted him. He wanted her. So what was there to talk about? Yet he still had that obdurate expression on his face, the one that told her the discussion would continue for as long as he needed it to.

"Why shouldn't it be right for both of us?" she asked, locking her hands around his wrists. "What could possibly be wrong with it?"

"Different goals, for one thing." He drew her closer and lifted his hands—and hers—to her neck, threading his fingers into her curls. She slid her hands to his elbows, loving the feel of the bulky muscles, the rough hair on his arms. There was something undeniably sexy about Rolph McKenzie's arms.

"I want a woman who is with me all the time, Marian. I want a permanent partnership. I told you that. House, yard, rosebushes, kids, the works. Things you don't want."

She dropped her hands from his arms and met his somber gaze. "But I do. I want that too. I know I've always said I didn't, but I've changed, Rolph. All the times I said that I'd never raise children, it was because I felt so shut out of my parents' lives. They've always been so connected. So together. I guess it was because for so long, it was just the two of them. You know they were married over twenty years before I was born."

"I know that. What difference does it make?"

"It made a difference to me. A big difference. I never felt there was room for me in the life they'd made for the two of them. Oh, I don't mean they didn't love me. They did. And they wanted me, but I think that once they had me, they didn't know quite what to do with me."

Rolph nodded. He'd always known what a lonely child Marian was. The rather wealthy, exclusive neighborhood they'd grown up in was comprised mainly of older, more established couples whose children had already left home. At eight years her senior, he'd been the closest to her in age. Many times, when he saw her leaning on the fence watching him and Max, he'd lifted her over so she could play too. Of course, she'd been too small to do most of the things they did, but he'd never minded letting her tag along.

"You and Max were great," she said, as if she'd read his thoughts. "All those times you took me places Mom and Dad were too tired to go to, or not interested in, like skiing, or out on your dad's boat, or to the exhibition every summer. But then, when you were away in college and I was sent to boarding school, I had to learn to fend for myself.

"I learned to be independent, not to let places and people matter all that much, because I wouldn't be staying. I thought it was best that way. Best for me."

Her expression made him think she'd long had serious doubts about what was best for her.

"It probably was," he said. "You aren't the kind to settle down, Marian. I even feel guilty some days about keeping you cooped up in the office. Whenever I see you gazing out the window, I think of how you'd be happier crewing on sailboats than spending your days buying and selling them for other people. For someone like you, that kind of work must feel like a trap."

"I like what I'm doing in your office," she said vehemently. "Sure, I enjoy getting out of doors a couple of times a day, but I don't feel cooped up or trapped in the office. And I wouldn't feel that way in a committed relationship."

"I was wrong," she went on. "Wrong about so many things. I told everyone I'd never have kids, because inside, I didn't want to have children who'd grow up the way I did, feeling lost and lonely and excluded from the magic circle. I realize now that most kids don't have those feelings, so there's no reason to think mine would. I guess, when I was saying things like that, it was a way of keeping myself from growing up."

She tried to smile, but only managed a crooked tilting of her mouth. "Whether I liked it or not, though, I did grow up. And now I want things I never thought I'd want. Like a home, babies. A husband."

He pulled her against him once more, enfolding her in his arms. She felt his heart pounding hard and fast in his chest. "Ah, sweetheart, now you say you want that, you might even think it's true, but what about six months from now? A year from now? Even five years from now? I don't think that is what you want, not in the long term. Your track record tells me that no matter what you say now, you're going to change your mind again. And likely again after that."

She pushed herself free of his embrace. "My track record? In two weeks you expect me to have established a track record?"

"Not two weeks. Your whole life. Remember, I've known you, watched you and all your changes since you were three years old. And yes, you've grown up, but your basic character hasn't changed, Marian. You're still as capricious, as variable as the winds, with mercurial moods. Sometimes you're completely down-to-earth and other times you float like a cloud. That's such a large part of your charm. It's what makes you an interesting, fascinating woman, and I'd hate to have you change. But it does not make you suitable for a guy who wants only to settle down. You'd be bored with a staid, sober businessman, and desperately unhappy. You're such a warm and sensitive person you wouldn't want to hurt him—me—by leaving, but your history tells me that you would leave. You'd have to."

"Why would I have to? And assuming you're right, and I found several years from now that I still wanted to travel, lots of people do. Couples travel together, they travel with their kids, they—"

"No," he said, laying two fingers over her lips. "I'm not talking about vacations in Disneyland. Let me finish, okay, because I'm talking about a way of life, your way of life. Look at it, at the way it's been, full and varied and interesting. I can't see you giving up all that and being happy. Not forever. You've flitted from school to school, from job to job, from business to business." He hesitated briefly. "A six-week marriage.

"Honey, you haven't exactly proved yourself stable. In fact, you've proved just the opposite, so for the two of us, I have to be the responsible one. I have to try to keep a cool head, to think things through before taking any irreversible steps. There always has to be one person in each relationship who does that."

She jumped to her feet, planting her hands on the overhead coaming to balance herself against the gentle bobbing of the boat. "And you figure it's your God-given male right to be that one? I let you get away with that kind of crap the other day, Rolph McKenzie, but not this time! When you were talking about 'the man' being the one to make the decisions, the one to 'be in charge,' that was one thing. Then, it was a nebulous, impersonal idea. But this is not. This is you and me, and I'm not prepared to listen to that kind of chauvinism or to have it applied to me and my relationship with you."

"Marian—"

"Excuse me. I'm not finished. I want you to know that when it came to my marriage, I was the responsible one! I was the one who tried to make it work! I was the one who went through hell when it was breaking up." Her voice cracked.

"Marian, don't. Don't talk about it. I'm sure you tried as hard as you could, but what depth can there have been to your commitment if you only tried for a few weeks?"

"You don't know a damned thing about it, Rolph McKenzie! Well, maybe that's my fault, because I've refused to talk about it. So fine, listen now, and I'll give you the gory details!"

Six

Rolph was repelled by the idea of hearing the details, gory or not. "No," he said quickly, sharply. Her marriage, as brief as it had been, was the last thing he wanted her to talk about. It made his insides crawl even to think of it. "I don't need to know about it. I don't want to know about it. A marriage that lasted a month and a half doesn't even merit discussion."

"Oh, yes, it does! And you're the one who brought it up. You're the one who called me irresponsible because of its short duration. What you don't know is that I did work at it! I tried to save it! I would have done anything to save it. I *did* everything. Even after I knew Wendell didn't love me, didn't even want me once he realized I wasn't a good meal ticket, I tried to work things out, because that was what was right." A spasm of pain crossed her face as she looked into a past that held more frustration and anguish than Rolph had even begun to suspect.

"Meal ticket?" he asked hollowly.

"Yes. That's what I was to him, but I didn't know it. I was naively convinced a man couldn't fake those kinds of feelings. I believed that since he wanted me physically, he must also love me. When he asked me to marry him, it never occurred to me that he wanted me for something other than the love I thought we shared. Then, when Mom and Dad cut off my allowance after I told them I'd gotten married, I was of no more use to him. A guy could get just as horny over a fat bankbook as he could over a cute tush, he told me, and it was my bankbook he really loved."

She pulled a wry face. "I didn't believe him. I stripped naked, both emotionally and physically. I spread my innermost feelings, my hopes and dreams, all over the place along with my clothes. The only thing I bared that stirred him in the least was my body. That he couldn't hide, but he still managed to walk away, leaving me feeling humiliated and cheap and unworthy."

She fixed Rolph with a straight gaze. "And stupid. The way I felt when you rejected me. I know you want me, but I know, too, that there's something else you want more. With him, it was money. With you, I don't know what it is."

Guilt was a physical pain in Rolph. "I wasn't rejecting you. If you're equating that scene with Wendell with what just happened between us, then stop. There is no comparison."

"No? I think there is. I threw myself at a man who was forced to decline, just as I did with Wendell. Then I could be excused due to my lack of experience and extreme youth. So I was pretty foolish, setting myself up for that again, wouldn't you say?"

"Marian—" he began, but she cut him off with a wave of her hand.

"I may be foolish, I may still lack judgment, but I am not irresponsible when it comes to my relationships. I never have been, so you have no right to call me capricious and irresponsible and inconstant because my marriage failed after only six weeks. You weren't there, Rolph. You have no way of knowing what it was like for me, and it's grossly unfair of you to judge me."

"You're right, and I apologize."

She stared at him. "What?"

"I said, you're right and I apologize. But," he went on, looking straight into her questioning eyes, "I still think that in our relationship, I'm going to have to be the one to take responsibility, to make sensible decisions." He paused deliberately. "To cool things when they get overheated, because it would be wrong for us to go ahead with it until we're certain it's going to work. For all time."

"You're asking for promises."

His gaze was steady. "Yes. I guess I am. And you can't make promises, can you?"

She thought about it, biting her lip. "What I can promise is that I will never, ever, set out to hurt you. I can promise that I believe right now, with all my heart, that you are what I want. I can promise that if I ever want to go away again, I'll come back to you. That is," she added in a rough whisper, "if you refuse to come with me when I go."

He was silent for a long time. When he spoke, she heard grief in his voice. "I don't know if that's good enough, Marian."

She turned from him, from the pain in his face. Hot tears squeezed past her tightly shut lids. "And so you won't take a chance on me because I might someday, want to do something else, be somewhere else, even temporarily?"

He caught her hand and pulled her back, seating her beside him on the berth. "I'm not saying that. I'm just saying I think we should exercise a little ·caution here, Marian. Lord knows I don't want to hurt you. But I don't want you to hurt me, either. The potential for emotional ruin is so great, it scares me to death."

She glared at him, her body tense, her chin high, her face flushed. She would have flown at him had he not held her with both hands on her arms. "Dammit, Rolph, life doesn't come with guarantees!"

Rolph knew she was right, but he also knew that with her he needed guarantees, promises, assurances. That she wasn't giving them only showed him how right he was to be wary of this building desire between them.

Yet a small part of him kept asking, what if she had changed? What if she could be as constant and faithful as he needed a woman to be? What if her feelings for him were as strong as his for her, or could become so? She claimed to want a commitment. Lord, but he wanted to believe that! Why was it so hard to believe?

Was this the love he'd been searching for? Had he found it in Marian? If he didn't reach out now and take it, was he risking throwing away everything he'd ever dreamed of, merely because he had doubts? Didn't every lover have doubts?

"How sure of this are you?" he asked finally, searching her eyes for the truth. "About what you feel for me."

She met his gaze squarely. "As sure as I've ever been of anything."

"No doubts?"

"Rolph . . . yes. I have doubts. It's normal to have them. I sometimes doubt my ability to make you happy. I doubt my sanity in wanting this so much, when I know that at any time you could turn from me, find someone else, someone who has all the characteristics you want in a woman. But I know that to get the gold, you sometimes have to dig through an awful lot of dirt." She touched his face. "What I do not doubt, though, is that being with you is what I want and need more than I've ever wanted or needed anything else. I believe that whatever potential our relationship—assuming we have one—has for pain, the possibilities are equally as great for joy. I guess you have to be something of a gambler to fall in love. I am."

Rolph continued to search her face for several seconds, then he shuddered and gathered her close. Drawing in her scent, he felt her heat, her trembling need. It echoed everything inside him. "I'll take a chance on you, sweetheart, if you'll take a chance on me."

Gently, he tilted her back so they both lay on the triangular bunk, crosswise of the boat. It was cramped and uncomfortable, but he wouldn't have traded it for a king's bedroom that didn't contain Marian. "I've wanted this since the day you came down to the marina and demanded a job."

She lifted a shaking hand and brushed it through his hair. "I've wanted this since Max and Jeanie's wedding. I think I've wanted it for a lot longer than that, but didn't know what it was I ached for. Now I know. Make love with me, Rolph."

"Yes," he said, his expression fierce with de-

sire and resolution. "I have to make love to you."
He captured her hands and held them together
over her head. "I have to have you now, and
again and again, but, Marian . . . I am not
going to fall in love with you." If he'd had the
breath to spare, he would have laughed at the
outrageous lie. But his breath stopped in his
lungs as Marian kissed him slowly and thoroughly, with his full cooperation.

"I'm not going to ask you for a commitment,"
he said moments later. He slid the T-shirt up
over her slender abdomen, then unhooked her
bra and pushed it aside. He gazed at her in avid
appreciation before bending his head and flut-
tering soft kisses up along the undersides of her
breasts. "When this . . . whatever it is, burns
itself out, you'll be free to go."

She gasped as his mouth fit over her nipple.
"It won't—burn itself out!" She arched her back.
"It won't. . . ."

Briefly, he lifted his head, his hand covering
one breast, gently rubbing its distended tip.
"Hush," he whispered. "Don't talk now. Just
kiss me like that again, and let me love you."

What was the point in arguing with him,
trying to convince him with words? Marian
wondered. There were other ways, and she was
willing to use every sweet one of them.

"Yes," she murmured. "Love me."

The feel of his body against her, the taste of
his mouth on hers, the scent of him in her
nostrils, combined to create a heady rush of
desire. Marian parted her lips for him, and he
kissed her as if starved for her, yet also gently,
softly, with an infinite tenderness that made her
ache deep inside like she'd never ached before.
She let her head fall back as he continued to

hold her hands, and opened herself more fully to him, feeling his tongue, the roughness of it, the hardness, as he searched out every sensitive spot within her mouth.

Moments later, he reluctantly lifted his head, met her slumberous gaze, and smiled. "Beautiful," he whispered.

"Rolph . . . please . . ."

"What, sweetheart? Tell me what you want."

"Don't stop . . . touching me."

"I won't. I can't. I want . . . this . . . so much."

He kissed her neck, her shoulder, her arm, then placed his hand on her lower abdomen, swirling caresses over her. Finally, in response to her wordless pleading, he curved his fingers in between her thighs, lifting her slightly as her legs fell apart. She murmured his name again, her eyes wide and dazed.

"Touch me," he ordered raggedly, at last letting her hands go.

She took the freedom he gave her gladly, greedily. Her hands traveled over his chest and down his sides, across his back, then inside the waistband of his blue shorts, creating convulsive tremors in each muscle she discovered.

Rolling away from her, he lifted the T-shirt off over her head and removed the rest of her clothing, then propped himself on one elbow. He traced the shapes of her breasts, the long, slender arc of her waist, the curve of her hip. His hand trembled as he parted the soft red hair between her legs, and his fingers found the slick moisture there.

"You are so beautiful," he said, and his voice trembled. He bent and kissed her breasts, drawing each of her nipples deep into his mouth and sucking hard, then more gently, flicking each one with the tip of his tongue before lifting his head again to smile at her. "And you taste so sweet, feel like satin."

Suddenly, he snatched her close, squashing her against his chest, rocking her as his hands swept over her back, her waist, her buttocks, driving her wild with need. "I can't get enough of you," he murmured. "There will never be enough."

She held him to her, their lips clinging together, and the power of their need ignited like a forest fire blazing up a windswept mountainside. "Rolph, now, hurry!" she cried, fighting to strip him naked as she was. Her hands got in his way, his interfered with what she needed to do, until it was done almost in spite of them. She sank back, drawing him down with her, one hand clasping the back of his head, holding his mouth to hers, the other curved around his hardness, stroking, loving, massaging. He pushed her hand away and parted her legs, surging into her with an urgent thrust. Knees lifted, her head flung back, her breath sucking in on a sharp, startled gasp, she took him into herself, wrapping him with her arms and legs, clinging as they both poised on the brink.

She opened her eyes, stared up at him, and said softly, "I love you, Rolph McKenzie."

With a groan, he buried his face against her neck. "I wish I could believe that!" he said. There was no more time for talking then, as the fire raged and consumed them both, then slowly, beautifully, burned itself out, until only occasional wisps of heat arose to let them know that embers remained within.

• • • •

"Marian?"

"Right here," she murmured, nuzzling her lips against his warm throat.

"I just had a thought."

She kissed his collarbone. "Me too. Was yours as good as mine?"

"Probably not, babe." He sounded unhappy, the last way she wanted him to feel, considering what had just happened between them. She lifted herself up on her elbows and looked down at him, concerned.

"There I was," he said, frowning, "talking all sorts of superior male stuff about responsibility and taking care of you, saying you needed protection and all that, and then I forgot to take care of the most important kind of protection of all. I'm sorry, honey."

She smiled. "And I told you I've been responsible in all my relationships. It's taken care of, Rolph. Don't worry."

He pulled her head back down to his shoulder and stroked her hair. "What did I do to deserve you?"

"I'm not sure how to take that," she murmured sleepily.

"As a compliment," he said. "Go to sleep."

Cuddled together, they both did.

"Rolph?"

"Hmm?" Slowly, he opened his eyes and looked over at the woman lying beside him. The woman he loved. The woman who had claimed, in a moment of passion, to love him. Light from the open hatch above them shimmered on her pearly skin. Her eyes were still closed and a smile curved her beautiful mouth. In another minute, he was going to find the strength to lean over and kiss that mouth.

"Would it be really rude," she murmured, "and horribly unromantic to tell you that I'm starving?"

He laughed. "Yes, considering what I'm thinking."

She opened her eyes and languidly ran her hand over his chest and shoulder. "What are you thinking?"

He shifted closer and watched her eyes widen, her smile deepen. "Oh!" she said, and moved her hand from his shoulder to his waist, then his hip. Her thumb made small, sneaky side trips, of which she appeared quite oblivious.

"Yes," he said, his breathing becoming ragged when her little forays became more deliberate. "'Oh!' is right."

She sat up and looked. "Ohhhh," she drawled, impressed. "I guess we're going to have to do something about that, aren't we? I mean, I understand it's terribly painful if left unattended?"

"Terribly," he agreed breathlessly, sending one of his hands on its own little trip of exploration, one that made her gasp and rise up onto her knees.

"Oh!" she said.

He grabbed her by the waist and lifted her astride him, fitting her down over him.

"Your vocabulary needs work, lady."

She smiled and leaned forward, her breasts brushing against his chin as she swayed back and forth. "No kidding. As long as it's my vocabulary and not my technique."

Sliding down, she stroked his nipples with a fingertip before bending and kissing each one, nibbling until he shuddered and lifted her up. "Your technique is fine. . . .

"My turn," he said, and captured one of her nipples in his mouth, holding her very still while he sucked for long, intense moments. He could feel her reaction to his caresses deep inside her where she held him in a velvet fist. He switched to her other breasts, and felt those inner convulsions recur.

"I can feel your response to that," he gasped. "It's incredible. You tighten all around me, quivering, and it's like heaven." With his thumbs, he stroked her wet nipples, then smiled as her muscles spasmed again. "Yes," he said. "Like that."

Again, she said, "Ohhh," on a long, drawn-out note as she dragged herself away from his greedy mouth, leaning back, her hands on his thighs, her head flung back. "Rolph!" she cried, and he tightened his hands around her waist, feeling the deep, hard shocks within her. Her legs tensed against him and she swayed, slowly at first, then faster, her wild rhythm infecting him. He rode the crest of passion with her until they were both sated, lying damp and replete in each other's arms.

"Hey, sleepyhead. A couple of hours ago you were starved. What about now?"

Marian rolled over and saw Rolph sitting beside her, dressed in his undershorts again. She laid a limp arm across her eyes to shield them from the sunlight slanting in through the main hatch while she assessed her degree of hunger.

"I just remembered," she said, coming more awake. "In my explorations earlier, about all I found was sardines. Believe me, I'd have to be an awful lot closer to starvation than I am now to eat them."

He smiled. "But you don't know what I can do with a can of sardines."

She sat up, reaching for her T-shirt, feeling inexplicably shy, maybe even inadequate. Through its fabric as she tugged it over her head, she said, "I don't care what you do with sardines. Nothing makes them edible." She grabbed his swim trunks and clambered into them.

"You'll see," he said. "Now come on. I put the dinghy in the water so we can go ashore and pick blackberries. You," he added loftily, "being the woman, get to make the pie."

"I," she said just as loftily, "happen to be a women who excels at making pies; therefore, I'll do so because I choose to."

He grinned. "And not because you were told to?"

"You got it," she said, shoving him out of her way. "Let's go, Tarzan."

A short while later, eyeing a can of asparagus that was the only vegetable aboard, Marian said, "I think I'll stick with pie for my dinner."

"Good little girls only get dessert if they eat up all their din-din," Rolph said. "You'll eat your rice and canned asparagus along with my magically transformed sardines, or you don't get pie."

Marian sat on the settee, her feet pulled up and her arms folded across her chest, watching Rolph as he filled a large pot with water and set it on top of the stove, then lit the burner under it. "Canned asparagus is almost as bad as your ugly, oily little fishes," she said. "But since I'm hungry, and you're my host, I'll make an exception and eat it. But only to be polite."

He set a lid on the pot, then turned and grinned at her. "You'd better be more polite about those 'ugly, oily little fishes,' or I might just refuse you even one tiny bite of the ambrosial transformation, my girl."

"Suits me," she said absently, hearing an echo of those words—my girl—as she watched him crouch to rummage in a locker. The last rays of the sun shone through a porthole, bronzing his golden hair and glinting off the stubble of beard forming on his chin. His muscles moved and worked under the smooth, tanned skin of his back and shoulders, and she wanted to touch him. Now that they were more or less dressed again, though, she felt a hint of distance between them. Not quite an awkwardness, but a reserve she'd been aware of since she'd wakened the last time. Was she really Rolph's girl? It was what she wanted to be more than anything in the world. But he had said he "had" to make love to her, as if he were compelled against his will. And he'd said he wasn't going to fall in love with her, so that it wouldn't hurt too badly when the whole affair "burned itself out."

Yet, deep inside where her innermost feelings lay, she was convinced he *did* love her. How could he have made love to her so sweetly, so tenderly, if he did not? And then she remembered Wendell.

"Hey, come on," he said, snapping her out of her reverie. "Don't look so sad. I didn't mean it."

She smiled at him and shrugged. "That's what I'm afraid of."

He gave her a questioning look, but let it drop, only reaching out to tousle her hair. "On deck with you, wench," he said, tugging her to her feet. "The bow deck." He reached for the book she'd been trying to read only a few hours before and tucked it under her arm. "Keep your nose buried in that. What I do to transmogrify those sardines is an old McKenzie family recipe and outsiders are never allowed to watch. I'll call you when dinner is ready." He kissed the tip of her nose, her chin, and then, hard and fast, her mouth, leaving her heart hammering painfully in her chest.

"No peeking," he ordered, shoving her toward the companionway. "Promise."

She nodded, her throat too tight with an intense ache to form words, and slipped out.

She didn't want to be an outsider. She wanted to be a loved and trusted member of the McKenzie family, the way Jeanie was. And after "whatever this was" finished "burning itself out," she didn't want to have to stand back and smile like a good, old friend while Rolph spent the rest of his life sharing *Sunrise VII* with somebody else.

Seven

Marian sat on the bow deck, facing forward, not reading the book on her lap. Instead her gaze roved along the outline of the long, low point that sheltered the bay from the sea's restless swells. Above her gulls dipped and wheeled and a single bald eagle soared in a high circle. She refused to give into despair. Dammit, she had won a round at least. Today she had *Sunrise*, and solitude, and Rolph. She was not going to give him up.

Unless, of course, those sardines proved to be his favorite dish. Then she might have to reconsider.

"All right, where are they?" Marian slid onto the settee and stared at her plate, on which lay a pile of rice beside several spears of asparagus covered with what looked suspiciously like cheese sauce. That made all the difference in the world. She could eat burned rope with cheese sauce. But of the despised little fishes, there was no sign.

Rolph grinned and flipped a tea towel—in lieu of a napkin—open on her lap. He sat across from her and covered his own lap. "Right here," he said, lifting the lid of the big pot and reaching in with another towel wrapped around his hand. With a flourish, he pulled out a large crab and set it on her plate so its bright orange pincers embraced the mound of rice. "I told you you wouldn't recognize them." He set another crab on his own plate.

"Oh, you rat, you," she said, catching on. "Old family recipe indeed! You used a can of sardines to bait your crab trap."

His grin broadened. "Works better than cat food. Besides, the sardines were free. A Norwegian client gave me a couple of cases." He wrinkled his nose. "Personally, I can't stand the ugly, oily little things."

"Well," she said, picking up one of the crab legs and snapping it free with a practiced twist of her wrist. "That's one thing we have in common."

"Only one?"

"How many do you think there are?"

He met her gaze, his own thoughtful. "We have a lot of things in common, honey."

"Yeah," she said. "The trick's going to be finding them."

He touched her wrist with a gentle hand. "We found a couple of them this afternoon, Marian. Or one of them, at any rate." He frowned. "An important one, I think."

She pulled her hand free. "Oh, I agree. Wholeheartedly."

He lifted his brows. "But?"

She shook her head and smiled, lightening the mood. "But nothing. Eat your sardines before they get cold."

It wasn't until much later, when they were taking an evening swim, that he brought up the subject again. Curling a hand around the nape of her neck, he turned her toward him as he held onto the anchor chain, the cool water of the bay swirling around them in fiery spiral of phosphorescence. Except for the fire in the water, it was dark, and he could see only the shape of her face, not her expression. She put her hands on his shoulders, let her legs float up around his waist, and snuggled close.

"Cold?" he asked.

"No. This is heavenly." He thought he caught the glimmer of her smile. "You're the first man I've ever skinny-dipped with."

Hands encircling her waist, he kissed her as they sank through the brilliance of the water, every movement sending shafts of light outward until Rolph kicked to surface again. Side by side, they floated on their backs.

"This is another thing we have in common," he said. "We both love the water, being either in it or on it."

She nodded. He felt the brush of her wet hair against his shoulder, and felt something else, too, something that had been bothering him since before dinner. A reticence, a reserve, an apartness from him when he thought they should be sharing a great closeness. She'd said she wanted him. He'd believe her. Hell, he still did. The kind of response she'd given him was not something any woman could fake.

But since then, her manner toward him had changed subtly, as if, having given of herself so generously, she was suffering regrets. "And it's good, what we share. Isn't it?" he asked.

"Of course it is." She swam away from him, lifted herself up the ladder at the stern and arose, silver water streaming down her lithe shape. She shook her head to rid her hair of droplets, and glowing splatters landed all around him in the moonless dark.

He joined her on deck, catching the towel she tossed him, and rubbed himself down before taking her towel and patting her skin dry with it.

He felt her erect nipples, sensed the change in her breathing, and knew they would be together again in only moments. "We have a lot going for us, don't we?" he murmured, letting both towels slip to the deck.

"Yes," she agreed, lifting her arms to encircle his neck. "Oh, yes."

As much as he wanted to consummate their union again, Rolph forced himself to hold back, to wait. As he had at dinner, he said, "But?" She went very still in his arms, wary, he thought, as if she might leap away if he didn't find a way to hold her.

"Why do you think there's a 'but'?" she asked.

It was an evasion and he knew it. Hands on her shoulders, he gave her a slight shake. "Because I know you, Marian. I sense a kind of distance in you, a holding back. You're not as happy as I'd like you to be."

"Oh, Rolph! Of course I'm happy," she said, but he knew from her tone that she was not.

"Marian, I'm not completely blinded by lust. Something's bothering you about this. About us. Can't you tell me what it is?"

This business of loving a man who had known her and cared about her since she was three years old was not going to be easy, Marian thought. With him, there would be—could be—no equivocation. She sighed.

"Suddenly," she said, "after we made love, after I discovered how wonderful it was to be living a dream come true, I realized it was my dream, not yours. And maybe it's not enough. Not enough for you. It's—I'm not what you're looking for. I hate to face it, but I know it's true."

"Not permanent, you mean?" He cupped her face in his hands. "Honey, I know that. I accept it. And when the time comes for you to move on, I won't hold it against you. Remember, I'm going into this with my eyes open. But I am going into it. You and I, together. It's what I want, for as long as we can have it."

"Sure," she said, stepping away from him. She wrapped one of the damp towels around herself like a sarong and sat on the stern seat. "And what happens when she does come along, your long-term lady? The one you want to take on an extended honeymoon, then bring home to the roses and the babies and the fences?"

He hesitated, the tremor in her voice hurting him, then sat down, the tiller between them. "What about her, Marian? I mean, assuming she even exists, she won't matter. Not to you. Because by then, you'll be gone." The idea of another woman there with him, aboard this boat or any other, was laughable. There would never be anyone but Marian. The thought of her leaving was painful, but he knew it would happen. As he'd told her, his eyes were open. He knew that Marian was not a sticker. He'd be a fool to hope for anything more than what he knew he'd get, and Rolph McKenzie was no fool.

She leaned over the tiller and clasped his arm in both of her hands, shaking him, her towel slithering to the seat behind her. "What if I don't want to go?" she demanded fiercely. "What if I never want to go? Will you spend the rest of your life secretly looking over your shoulder to see if she's in sight, that perfect woman of yours, the one who can make all kinds of rash promises and guarantees—the kind of promises you'll believe?" She drew a deep breath and crawled over the tiller, kneeling beside him, splaying her hands on his chest. "Rolph, if you're willing to believe her, whoever and wherever she is, why aren't you willing to believe me?"

He pulled her onto his lap, cradled her head in his hands, and kissed her long and hard. Together, they rose and stumbled below, sliding onto the berth, clinging to each other.

"Whoever and wherever she is," Rolph said, "she doesn't belong in this bed with you and me. I told you, as long as you're with me, I won't be looking for her, over my shoulder secretly or in front of my nose, openly. As long as I have you, I don't want anybody else. Now shut up and kiss me, because that's what's important right now. And when you're doing that, I can't be looking over my shoulder, now, can I?"

She shut up and kissed him, but her heart ached because he still hadn't said why he found it so impossible to believe in her. What more was she going to have to do to show him that she truly loved him?

Just as Rolph couldn't look over his shoulder

while she was kissing him, Marian found that her heart couldn't ache while he was kissing her. So she close the path that drew her like a magnet, deep into ecstasy with him.

"You still don't have any furniture!" Marian stood, hands on hips, looking around Rolph's barren living room.

"What do you call that?" He gestured at the desk and chair in one corner of the room, near the patio doors. "And this?" He nudged open another door with his foot and showed her a bedroom with a dresser, a king-size bed, and a large-screen TV with a VCR on top.

The kitchen contained a card table and two folding chairs, which was the only major improvement since he'd showed her around that first day.

"I thought this was your home," she said. "How can you live like this? I mean, you own this place. You should own furniture. At least enough to make you comfortable."

He gave her a look. "Do you?"

"Well, no. My apartment was furnished when I moved in and there didn't seem to be any point in getting my own. I don't know how long I'll be in it."

He shrugged. "Then how can you complain about my not having furniture?"

"If I owned a home, I'd own its furnishings."

"I have what I need," he said. "I'll get the rest . . . sometime."

Oh. Of course, she thought. She knew when. When he found that paragon he wanted. Of course he wouldn't buy furniture now. Whoever and wherever his wonder-woman was, she'd want to choose. But living the way he did was nothing short of ridiculous, Marian thought. He didn't even have a place to sit and relax, a place to entertain his friends—

Through the open door, she saw that king-size bed and huge television. It told her a lot about where Rolph entertained. She glared at the room, then deliberately turned away from it. It was still there, though, and she was aware of it in a way she didn't like. Over her shoulder, she took another look. It was still as . . . decadent as it had been five seconds ago, that big bed, the television angled just so for easy viewing, the VCR suggesting rented videos. What kind? she wondered. The kind Wendell had always liked to watch before and even during sex? She whirled and marched toward the room to close the door.

Before she got there, Rolph slipped his arms around her from behind, pulling her against him. "Hey, what's the matter?" he asked.

"Nothing," she said, turning in his embrace. "I—I think I'm ready to go home. I mean, now that I have shoes on my feet again, I feel I can face the world." Some kind soul had brought her shoes up from the wharf where she'd kicked them off, and left them beside her desk.

"You're the only person I know who's comfortable facing the world in purple shoes," he said.

She burrowed against him. "Come home with me, Rolph."

Lifting her head, he searched her face with his intense gaze. "Marian," he said after a moment, "no woman has ever been in that bed in there with me. And no woman ever will, except you, as long as you and I are together. That's a promise."

She blinked. "I— Dammit, how did you know?"

"Because, my sweetheart, you have the most readable face in the world. Those suspicious, resentful glances you kept shooting at my bed told me all I needed to know." He brushed his lips over her eyelids, her cheeks, her mouth. "Will you share it with me tonight?"

She smiled. "And any other night."

He swung her up in his arms and strode into his bedroom. When he deposited her in the middle of the mattress, it sloshed and gurgled for a moment before settling down. Its warmth seeped into her back while he divested her of her purple shoes. "I guess," he said as he joined her on the bed, "I'm going to have to out and pick up a few more pieces of furniture. We might get tired of the bed. A sofa would be nice, and a recliner, or maybe a love seat. Maybe both, and a big, shaggy rug to lay in front of the fireplace."

She unbuttoned his shirt and ran her hands through his chest hair. "This is all the shaggy rug I need."

He grinned. "And you're what I want to lay. In front of the fireplace or anywhere. Any time."

His whiskers were a sharp bristle against her neck, but Marian didn't mind. "Okay," she murmured. "Do it."

It was dawn when he woke her. Waving a cup of coffee under her nose, he drew her from sleep. Marian opened her eyes to see the dappled light of the harbor bouncing around the room. That one glance was more than enough. She squeezed her eyes shut, rolled onto her stomach, and hid her face in the pillow. "Go away. It's the middle of the night."

"The sun's up."

"It's summer, silly. The sun gets up in the middle of the night in these latitudes."

"Five o'clock is morning to most people."

"Only to torturers who don't fully qualify as people. Leave me alone." She wriggled as he drew the sheet back and ran a fingernail down the length of her spine.

"I," he said, "am a morning person. Don't tell me you aren't?"

"I aren't."

He kissed the back of her neck. "You were yesterday."

"That was different. Night sort of blended into morning, and we spent half the day sleeping because we hadn't spent much of the night doing it."

He chuckled. "The way I remember it, we did spend most of the night doing it."

"Sleeping!" she wailed. "What I want to do now."

He picked her up, then carried her into the bathroom and into the shower, where he held her as she squalled and fought and kicked, but the cold water had the desired effect. Marian woke up.

Dripping wet, she glared at him when he stood her in the middle of the bathroom floor. "You'll regret that, McKenzie. When I don't get enough sleep, I'm mean and ugly and of very uncertain temper."

"You haven't got a mean bone in you, you're too beautiful to be ugly, and you've always had an uncertain temper. But luckily, I learned—recently—how to sweeten you, so why should I worry?" He grinned. "Come here. Want me to make you sweet?"

"I want you to let me go back to sleep."

"No, you don't. You're wide awake now." He wrapped her in a big towel and rubbed her back. "Sweetheart, as much as I'd love to keep you captive in my bed for the rest of—for a long time, we have to face facts. Before long, this entire marina is going to be awake and I want you safely out of here before that happens."

She stared at him. "Why? Rolph—"

He laid a finger over her lips. "Hush. I know what you're going to say. We slept together. You aren't ashamed of that. You don't care who knows. Well, I'm not ashamed of it either, but I do care who knows."

He gestured to where her slacks, blouse, and jacket hung neatly on a hanger. "Two days ago, you came to work wearing that very distinctive outfit. You were seen boarding my boat wearing it." He grinned and looked down at her feet. "Or most of it. If you're seen leaving this morning in the same clothes, everyone will know perfectly well that you spent last night and the night before with me, and I won't have you the butt of any dirty male jokes."

"That's a wonderful sentiment," she said, stepping out of his embrace. "Beautifully, eloquently put. Too bad I don't believe one single word of it."

"What—"

She shoved him through the bathroom door. "Out!" She shut the door and locked it. He hammered on it. "Go away. I'm doing what you want. I'm getting dressed. " She pulled on her underwear, her slacks. "Then I'll leave. Quietly, of course, carrying my ghastly shoes and tiptoeing so that I don't alert anyone to my presence here at this unseemly hour." After hooking her bra, she jammed her arms into the sleeves of her silk blouse and buttoned it, then grabbed her jacket. She opened the door.

Rolph stood there waiting, blocking her way.

She shoved him again. "Move."

"Oh, hell, you're misunderstanding me completely!"

"I don't think so. I understand this much. You have no intention of going public with our relationship."

"To protect you, Marian!"

"Oh? And what if I don't want to be protected?"

She swung away from him, picked up her shoes, and stepped out onto the deck. He followed her, his eyes blazing with indignation as he spun her around to face him. "You have to be protected. The guys who live down here can be animals. Given half a chance, they make mincemeat of a nice girl's reputation. Dammit, they're bachelors!"

She laughed. "So are you."

He looked startled. "But . . . that's different. I don't indulge in locker-room gossip. I won't talk about you. I won't—"

"Acknowledge publicly that you and I are lovers."

He looked unhappy. He also looked stubborn. "No, I won't."

"Okay, then. I will." Before he could stop her, she whirled away and ran to the railing. "Good morning, Sunrise Marina! My name is Marian Crane and I am Rolph McKenzie's lover!"

A startled great blue heron flew off a barnacle-encrusted piling with a noisy flapping of wings. A hatch popped open three boats away and a head poked through.

Marian waved her shoes. "Good morning!" she

called. "It's a beautiful day and Rolph McKenzie woke me up so we could enjoy it together!"

The man laughed and waved back, said something she couldn't hear, and stepped out onto the wharf. He was joined by a woman who stared up at Marian and Rolph. Marian waved at the woman, too, then at a little child in a yellow life jacket, who sidled out from behind a piling and gaped up at her.

"Have you ever been in love?" she called down to him. The boy shook his head, his eyes big and brown in his suntanned face. "Just wait," she said. "It's wonderful! You'll adore it when it happens to you."

Rolph was torn between embarrassment and amusement. "Marian, be quiet!" He tried to swing her away from the rail.

She grinned at him and dropped her shoes, one at a time, to land with two distinct "thunks" on the wharf twenty feet below. One bounced overboard with a splash. The little boy ran along the float, bare feet thudding, and fished it out. His passage brought another couple of heads out of hatches, another person or two out on decks.

"It's a wonderful day to be in love," Marian told them, and they made appropriate comments, accompanied by huge smiles and resigned, amused shakes of their heads.

Marian danced across Rolph's deck, singing the opening lines to "Oh, what a beautiful morning" in a clear yet throaty voice that surprised Rolph. He hadn't heard her sing since she was a child. It crossed his mind that *he* was the one who'd made her sing and that had to count for something, but his embarrassment kept growing, blocking out any sort of philosophical

thought. He just wanted her to stop this foolish-
ness. When she finished the verse and bowed to
the applauding audience below, an audience
that had grown to alarming proportions, he
knew it was past time to go.

As they walked along the wharf toward the
parking area, people greeted them. A few made
arch comments, and Rolph growled answers.
His face turned red when Marian sunnily assured the boaters that not everyone was a morning person, and promised to feed him breakfast
and bring him back in a better mood.

On the esplanade along the harbor shore, she
again began to sing, swinging Rolph's hand
between them. Early strollers glanced at them,
smiled, then looked away.

"Would you be quiet?" he begged, after an
elderly man actually stopped and stared at
them.

She spun into his arms. "Probably not without inducement," she said, pouting saucily.

Rolph felt caught on the cusp between fury
and mirth. She stood there, gazing up at him,
her eyes filled with mischief, the sun creating a
halo in her hair. She was sunshine and morning and girlhood dressed up as a woman. She
had him totally captivated, charmed, enchanted, and bemused, and there wasn't a damned
thing he could do about it . . . except "induce"
her to be quiet.

"See?" she said breathlessly several moments
later. "That wasn't so difficult, was it?"

"No," he said, surprised at exactly how easy it
had been to show the world that he wanted this
incredible woman. "No," he said again, and
started laughing, laughing at her, at himself,
but more important, laughing *with* her. Lean-

ing against the rail, holding her, he was over-come with hilarity that welled up out of nowhere and went on and on. "Lord almighty," he said, pulling her closer. "I don't know what I'm going to do with you."

She leaned back, her grin total provocation. "I'm sure you'll think of something."

She watched his eyes darken and his smile fade, and felt his breath hot on her cheek. "I have," he said raggedly. "But it starts with getting you home."

"Race you," she said, darting away toward the parking lot. She was already in her car when he caught up with her. He stood at her door, and she saw his mouth form the words, "One of these days . . ."

She rolled down the window. "One of these days, what?"

He blew out a long breath, rolled his eyes heavenward, then laughed again as if he couldn't help himself. "Just drive, lady. I'll follow you."

Marian took the quickest route home, with Rolph's car close behind.

"We have to get up and go to work," she said some time later, rolling to a half-sitting position and tickling his ear with a small feather from her pillow. "Besides, I promised the gang at the marina I'd feed you breakfast to put you in a better humor."

"You put me in a wonderful frame of mind without breakfast."

"Still, we have to get up."

"I know." He glanced at the clock on the bedside table. "But it's only eight o'clock."

She flopped back down. "I can't believe this! Eight is the time I normally get up, and I've been awake for three hours."

He chuckled. "But look how productive those hours have been. You know what they say about the early bird."

She rolled her head toward him and gave him a slow, all-encompassing look. "I ain't seen no worms."

"Thank you kindly for that, ma'am."

"You know, I always thought it was only in fiction that a man could—" She broke off as the phone rang.

"Hello?" she said, then her eyes widened as she stared at Rolph in dismay. She pulled the sheet up to her chin. "Oh, uh, hi, Mom. How are you? Who, me? I'm fine. Just . . . fine. I . . . uh, no, nothing's wrong. I do? Really, Mom, I'm fine. Yes, of course I'm alone! I'm sorry. I was away. On business."

Rolph stretched out an arm and ran his hand up the inside of her thigh. She shifted her leg out of harm's way. He followed her, sliding out on her side of the bed when she did. She turned her back on him and curled in a chair, holding the phone close to her face in a protective, secretive manner.

"Well, yes," she said to her mother, "with Rolph. Mom, he's not a man!" She jerked erect as Rolph reached around her and cupped a breast in one hand, tweaking a nipple. "Ouch!" she muttered.

"I mean," she went on into the phone, "he's not a man-man. He's my boss. I have to go on business—" She stared at Rolph for an instant. His eyes were closed, his mouth soft on her breast. He was certainly enjoying himself. "Trips with him sometimes." Her voice squeaked. He lifted his head, smiled sweetly, and kissed her neck. Her breath caught.

"What? What did you say, Mom? Of course I haven't forgotten Dad's birthday is a week from next Saturday. Certainly. I'll remind him this morning when I get to . . . when I get to . . . work. What? I'm sorry. I didn't meant to sound distracted. I just woke up. Well, you know I'm not"— Rolph nuzzled the phone cord aside and nibbled on her shoulder—"at my best in the . . . morning. Oh, Lord . . ." She covered the phone and hissed, "Stop that!"

"No, Mom, truly, I wasn't talking to anybody. Well, just my cat. I . . . yes. Yes, I have a cat. I got it, uh, last week. It's a kitten, really, and it sometimes chews on my . . ." She curved her hand around Rolph's chin, trying to remove him from her breast, but he wasn't to be swayed from his task. "Uh, my toes. It . . . tickles and—Mom, can I call you back? Fluffy needs her litter box and the bathroom door is shut."

"Fluffy?" Rolph said, laughing as he flopped back onto the bed, carrying her with him. "Surely you could do better than that?"

"I'm going to kill you," she said, kneeling astride him. "I'm going to cut you up into little, bitty pieces and . . . and . . . Oh!"

"And?" he prompted her, teeth flashing, eyes glittering.

"And, well, kill you," she whispered helplessly as he thrust upward with his hips.

"You probably are," he murmured against her throat. "But what a way to go."

Eight

"Why didn't you tell your mother I was at your place?" Rolph asked as he and Marian walked from the parking lot toward the marina at half past nine.

She'd been waiting for the question, and knew, in light of her earlier actions there at the marina, that it was justified. Trouble was, she didn't have an adequate answer for him.

"I guess . . . because if she knew we were, well, seeing each other, she'd get her hopes up or something."

"And you don't want to raise unrealistic expectations?"

With a sidelong glance at him, she nodded. "Something like that." In a rush, she added, "Rolph, I'm sorry for what I did this morning. I understand now why you wanted to keep our relationship private. I can see that you're right. Whatever is happening between us should remain just between us. It's too uncertain, isn't it, for sharing?"

He put his arm around her, bumping up against her a time or two. It was too brotherly a gesture for her liking. "For now, honey," he said. "At least outside of the marina." He shrugged. "Here, I'm afraid, our cover is blown."

"I said I'm sorry."

He lifted one of her hands to his mouth and kissed it. "As far as the marina goes, I'm not. In fact, I think it's best this way. You know I've never been comfortable about your wandering around here unprotected. This way, every sea-going wolf knows it's strictly hands-off, because the lady is Rolph McKenzie's girl." He grinned. "She said so herself. At the crack of dawn. Very, very publicly."

He looked, she thought, positively smug. She wasn't certain she liked that.

"The lady," she said, slipping her hand free of his clasp, "doesn't require protection."

He draped an arm around her shoulders. "Too bad. She's got it."

Before entering the outer office of the broker-age, he removed his arm. "Listen," he said, frowning slightly. "I hate to say this, but I have to. About us working together. Once we go through this door, what's happened between us is forgotten until after hours. It has to be that way. Can you live with that?"

She met his gaze. "Of course. I wouldn't want it any other way. Professionalism, Rolph, all the way."

"Good, then. We're in agreement."

He touched her shoulder, then trailed his hand down her arm to her fingers. His eyes looked somber, but she smiled at him and his expression lightened. Bending, he kissed her swiftly on the mouth. "Why," he asked, "do I get the feeling you're going to find this 'profession-alism' stuff easier than I am?"

As she entered the big, sunlit office she shared with Rolph and saw the stacks of papers on both their desks, the yellow phone message slips, and thought about the work waiting for her in her briefcase, Marian didn't think either she or Rolph were going to have any difficulty attending strictly to business. They weren't going to have time for anything else.

Rolph broke his own rule briefly just before he left for the airport for his delayed meeting in Seattle. Coming up behind her as she started to make yet another call, he tilted her chair back and kissed her long and hard.

"I'll call you tonight," he said, looking deep into her eyes. "And I'll miss you like mad. Plan for a long, leisurely lunch tomorrow." His eyes darkened to smolder sexily. "At your place."

She sighed. "I'd love to, but I have a lunch meeting tomorrow with Al Gunderson."

Rolph straightened. "Why does it have to be a lunch meeting? There's no need for you to work through your lunch hour."

"There's every need. That's the only time he's free. I want to show him that Camano 28 the Freisans are selling."

"I don't like it," Rolph said.

"Listen," she said, standing to slug this out with him. "You've never objected to my meeting clients for lunch before, and you do it all the time. What do you want me to do, start refusing them simply because you want me to go home and do a little secret snuggling with you?"

He frowned unhappily. "If that's the way you want to put it, yes. It's a case of priorities. Who's more important to you, a client or me?"

She bristled. "I can't believe I heard that. This is professionalism? I am having lunch with Al Gunderson, who came to this company in search of a boat because he's a lifelong friend of my father's and he wants to help my career. I refuse to insult him because you're being irrational, and I also refuse to deny myself the commission you'll owe me if this sale goes through."

"Al Gunderson, Senior?" Rolph asked.

Marian arched an eyebrow. "And if it had been Al Gunderson, Junior?"

"I—" He blew out a long stream of air. "All right. Sure. Professionalism. We don't cancel lunch dates with clients so we can spend an hour or two in your snug little bed, do we?"

"Not if we want to keep our clients, we don't," she said, and touched his face with her hand. "Rolph, please trust me. I don't want any man but you. Now go on. Get out of here or you'll miss your plane. See you tomorrow."

To Rolph's disappointment, Marian wasn't in the office when he arrived home the next afternoon, but she called twenty minutes after he'd sat down at his desk. She was reporting on a transaction she had underway, she said, but he knew she'd only called to hear his voice, and he kept her talking simply to hear hers. He sat there smiling, listening to the lilt of her tone, loving the sound of it, the way it infiltrated his being and vibrated in his bones. It wasn't until she let out an angry yelp that he started really hearing her words again.

"What the *hell*?" she exclaimed. "Hey! You! Wait!"

"Marian! What's wrong?"

"That guy's stealing my car! Taxi! Taxi!"

"No!" Rolph shouted. "Don't follow him! Call the police! Where are you? Wait for me! Marion!"

But all he heard was her shrill whistle and the monotonous thud, thud, thud as the phone she'd apparently thrown down swung on its cord.

"Marian!" he yelled uselessly into the phone again, then slammed it down. Bursting into the outer office, he demanded to know where Marian had just been, and where she was expected next, and when. She was in danger and he didn't even know where she was, but somehow, he had to get to her.

Unfortunately, neither Kaitlin nor Andrea could say where she was, either, because she had been in transit between appointments that were on two opposite sides of town. There was nothing he could do.

"Oh, God. Oh, God," he said as he paced the outer office, his heart hammering, waiting, waiting, waiting for a call that never came. "What's happening? Where is she? What is she doing?" In those moments, he realized exactly how much she meant to him.

Marian flung herself into the front seat of the cab that pulled up in response to her two-fingered whistle. "That's my car up there!" she yelled. "The blue one. Some kid just stole it. Follow it." She dug in her bag and found a twenty and a ten. "Can you catch him?"

"If I can't, the cops can." As the driver peeled out after Marian's car, now two blocks ahead and turning left through a very small break in traffic, he was also busy on his radio to his dispatcher. He gave times, directions, and a description of her car, which Marian fed him as he talked. All the while he drove with one hand, easily, relaxed, not speeding but wasting no time. He was a much more experienced driver than the young thief, and within ten blocks was abreast of Marian's car.

She leaned out her window as the taxi driver gave a long, angry blast of his horn. "The police are on their way!" she shouted at the boy. "You better pull over and give me back my car or—"

It was too late for the boy to do anything else. From several different directions, police cars converged, sirens whining, lights flashing. The badly shaken youth pulled to the curb, then got out with his hands up and his face white with terror. It was all over in a few minutes. After giving her statement, paying the cab driver, and getting thoroughly lectured by an officer about leaving her keys in the ignition while she stopped "only for a minute" to make a phone call, Marian was on her way again.

She was tired as she walked back to her car after her last appointment of the day, but her spirits lifted as she saw Rolph striding toward her. Surprised that he'd come to her instead of waiting for her to return to the marina, she hurried to meet him. "Hi!" she said, smiling. "I missed you. What—"

"Why in the hell didn't you call me?" he demanded, planting himself squarely in front of her on the sidewalk. "I went out of my mind until the cops finally told me you had your car back, they had the kid, and everything was all right."

"But—"

"But everything was not all right, Marian! *I* was not all right!"

"Rolph—"

Words poured from him as he clamped her shoulders, his fingers biting into her flesh. "I have never been so scared in my life!" he went on furiously. "There was some guy swiping your car in broad daylight, so I knew he was crazy or on drugs, and there you were, whistling down a cab so you could follow him!"

He gave her a little shake. "How could you be so half-witted to take off on your own after a car thief? I told you not to. I told you to wait for me. I told you—"

She shoved his hands away and stepped in close, angry now herself. "You wait just one minute there, bub!" she said sharply. "What gives you the right to manhandle me? And what's this 'I told you' garbage? I'm a grown-up, Rolph. You don't tell me what to do except in the office!" She poked him in the chest with a stiff finger. "I did what I saw as the best thing under the circumstances. I had to make the decision and there was no time to consult anybody, especially a guy who was sitting in an office all the way across town. It was my car being stolen, and I was on the scene, so I had to act. I did, and events proved me right, so what's your beef?"

"My 'beef,' as you put it," he said, grabbing her finger, "is that you scared me out of my mind, that you didn't wait for me to come and help you, and you didn't call back to tell me you were all right. I've suffered more agony this afternoon than I ever have in my entire life!"

Suffer? Scare? Call? Marian suddenly realized that if he was angry now, it was the kind of anger that follows extreme fright. Fright she could have eased with a simple, two-minute phone call.

"Oh, Rolph," she said, turning her hand in his and bending her head to kiss his knuckles. She looked up into his snapping eyes and saw there the residue of terror. "I'm sorry, love," she said contritely, sliding her arms around him and holding him close. "I didn't mean to be thoughtless. It never occurred to me that you'd be worried."

She felt terrible for having frightened him so badly. Leaning back from him, her arms still around his middle, she said, "I'm not used to having anybody to call and I was late for my appointment down here, so I was in a hurry. I guess I wasn't thinking. I should have realized the way I ended my call to you sounded . . . well, alarming."

He wasn't so easily placated. "Alarming? It sounded downright dangerous. As I saw it, you were tearing off in a cab to tackle a car thief all alone."

She had to protest that. "Come on, Rolph. You must have known I wouldn't have tried anything so dumb. You heard me whistle for the cab. You knew I wasn't alone. All taxis have radios, and of course he called the police, so I was never in any danger."

"All right, I did know that," he conceded. "At least on one level. But for quite a while, that level wasn't on top. What bothers me, I guess, is that you went to somebody else, a stranger, for help."

She frowned. "But that's silly. The taxi driver was in a better position to help than you were. I didn't mean to upset you, though. It wasn't deliberate. I simply didn't think about it. If I'd been on the phone to somebody else, you never would have known my car was stolen until I got back to the office. But you're right. Since you did know, I should have called you back." She smiled. "Forgive me?"

He pulled a wry face. "Of course. Just don't be so damned independent all the time."

"But I am independent, Rolph. I don't think I can change that. I've always looked after myself, made my own decisions." She let his hand go and locked hers around her shoulder bag. "I don't think I can give it up," she said seriously, with perhaps a note of warning in her tone. "It cost me too much to earn it."

He thought of her marriage, of her lonely childhood, and knew the cost she spoke of. "I know, but I worry about you," he said, cradling her face in his hands. "You are very, very important to me, Marian Millicent, and you're going to have to remember that. You'll also have to remember that you aren't alone anymore."

She smiled. "I'll try. If I forget, feel free to remind me."

"Like this?" he whispered, and she sighed in response, arching her neck as he kissed her throat.

"Not here," she said, and reluctantly he agreed. But he followed her back to the office very carefully, lest something happen to her on the way.

"What do you want for dinner tonight?" he asked much later. "Italian? Vietnamese? Indian?"

She thought about it for a moment, then

shook her head. "How about regular Canadian?"

He looked startled. "Steak?"

"Sure," she said with a grin, "as long as it's my favorite kind—ground, flattened into a patty, and stuck inside a bun with a bunch of gooshy sauces, some bacon and cheese, and a heap of fries beside it."

"You want a hamburger?"

His surprise surprised her. "Why not? I love them."

Hand in hand they walked down the ramp to the wharf. "I never would have guessed that about you," he said. "I mean, if anybody had asked me what I thought one of your favorite meals would be, I'd have come up with something exotic and foreign. All those places you've been, I'm amazed you didn't discover something a lot better than a burger and fries."

"Well," she said, as they began the ascent to the parking lot level, "I have to confess to one other choice that sometimes wins out over burgers."

At the top, he swung her around to face him, his arms curved around her back. "And what's that? If it's available in this town, you've got it, lady."

"Peanut butter and banana sandwiches."

He laughed and hugged her, then kissed her for several minutes until somebody down in the marina blew a boat's horn and another kibitzer whistled long and loud. Releasing her, Rolph turned and bowed deeply, then took her hand again, walking toward his car. "Now," he said, "let's be serious for a few minutes here. In all your travels, didn't you find one nation's food better than any other?"

"Yes," she said. "Ours. Like most people, I prefer what I grew up with, such as hamburgers, fried chicken, and seafood. And salads. There were times, particularly in Italy, when I would have killed for a nice, fresh salad. I lived in a rooming house and my landlady didn't know a head of lettuce from a mountaintop. I'd see all those incredible, fresh, red, ripe tomatoes in the markets and drool. Sometimes, I'd buy a few and sneak them into my room and eat them like apples. Yet all she did was cook them. And broccoli. She cooked that until it was thoroughly dead." She grinned as he opened the car door for her. "You know something? I never even found a good pizza in Italy."

"Sure," he said, enchanted and amused. "And I've heard people say you can't get good Chinese food in China."

"That," she said, "is completely true." He shut her door and walked around the car to get in behind the wheel. "But," she continued, "I wouldn't want to give the impression that I'm one of those travelers who hates everything that's not exactly the same as it is at home. I've had some fantastic meals in many different places and I'm always happy to try something new. Like reindeer steak in Lapland, though I felt a little guilty thinking about Santa and Rudolph and 'each little hoof.'"

He pulled out into the street. "Where haven't you been?" he asked with a nearly silent sigh.

"Oh, hundreds of places," she said. "We live in such a big world, Rolph, and there are so many wonderful corners of it waiting to be explored."

Faraway places . . . "And you mean to explore every one of them." It was not a question.

She shot him a quick glance. His face was set

into a mask of stiff lines. "No!" she said quickly. Seeing him frown, she realized her response had been too swift, like an answer given by rote, with no thought behind it. "Maybe someday I'd like to do more traveling, Rolph, but it's not all wonderful, you know. There are advantages to being at home." She touched the back of his hand as it rested on the wheel.

"Such as?"

"People I care about. Familiar food." She paused for a beat. "Nice toilets."

To her relief, his frown faded and he flashed her a quick smile. "Not necessarily in that order?"

"Right." She laughed. "Now, it's your turn. What's your favorite food?"

"Well," he said ponderingly, "we've eliminated sardines. . . ."

Marian actually thought Rolph was beginning to trust her, to believe that she wasn't planning to run away at the first opportunity, when the call came from the Mastersons in Australia, two weeks after their dinner at Estevan's.

"Marian. Hi, sweetie." Marian beamed as she heard Ethel's distinctive voice on the line. "Is Rolph there too? Good, put this on speaker, will you? We have great news we want to share with you."

This was the first call they'd had since Ethel and Slim had flown to Australia to check out *Catriona*. Marian could tell by Ethel's bubbling enthusiasm that the boat was all they'd hoped for. "Rolph, listen up," she said, and flipped on the speaker.

"*Catriona*'s as beautiful as we'd remembered!"

Ethel's voice boomed into the office. Marian adjusted the volume. "We took her out today for her first sea trials."

"Already?" Rolph asked. "That was quick."

"She turned out to be in better shape than we'd dared to hope, though she'll need a bit of time in dry dock to replace a few defective planks," Slim responded. He spoke in technicalities for several minutes while Rolph murmured replies and took a few notes. "We had her out under power, of course," Slim went on. "The new sails won't be ready for at least another two months, and we'll be replacing all of her masts before that."

"I can't wait to see her under sail," Marian said, smiling. "Send me miles and miles of videotape. What a dream come true it'll be, seeing her the way I used to imagine her when she was tied up to that dock selling seashells and machine-made scrimshaw."

"Why bother with videotapes?" Slim said. "Come on down and see for yourself."

"Lord! Wouldn't I love to!" she exclaimed. She turned to Rolph, her smile broadening. "Rolph—"

He abruptly shoved his chair back and shot to his feet. "Sorry, folks," he said. "I have an appointment I can't miss. Talk to you later. Glad everything's going so well. Keep in touch." With that, he snatched up his briefcase and jacket and strode from the office, leaving Marian to stare after him and somehow continue the conversation with the same level of enthusiasm with which she'd started it. What in the world had gotten into him? she wondered. His face had been almost white, he'd gone so pale. He hadn't met her eyes, and had run out of there as if the place were on fire. When she asked Kaitlin and Andrea where he'd gone, neither had any idea.

Rolph returned at five-thirty, as Marian was preparing to leave for home. He entered the office, closing the door quietly behind him. Leaning against the door, he looked at her.

"Well?" he said. "When do you want to go?"

She drew in a deep breath and let it out slowly. She'd long since figured out why he'd run. If only she hadn't greeted Slim's suggestion that she come see the ship with such delight. Of course, Rolph, with his awful lack of faith in her, had thought she was on the verge of leaving.

She managed a tiny smile. "I'm not going anywhere, Rolph. Remember? I have a contract here that still has a while to run."

He shook his head impatiently and pushed away from the door. "Look, that contract's not important and we both know it."

Her hands clenched at her sides. "It's important to me, Rolph, but there's something that's a whole lot more important. You. Our relationship. I don't want to leave you. I don't intend to leave you."

He walked forward, dropping his briefcase beside his desk, until he was within arm's reach of her. He didn't touch her.

"No," he said. "Maybe you don't. Not right now. But dammit, Marian, you will. I saw that look on your face! I saw the longing, the excitement, the eagerness, when the Mastersons asked you to come aboard."

"All right, for a moment or two, I thought of

how wonderful it would be to see *Catriona* under sail, to watch her with a bone in her teeth, to stand on her decks and feel her response to the ocean and wind, listen to her timbers creak. You'd love it, too, Rolph, and that's what I was picturing, you and me there . . . together. The invitation wasn't only for me. It was for both of us, as you'd have learned if you'd stayed for another two minutes."

"Maybe it sounded that way," he said, weariness and defeat in both his voice and his eyes. "But we both know—and the Mastersons know—I'm not free to leave. I have a marina to manage and a brokerage to run. You're the one they want, the one who interests them. Your background is perfect for their purposes. You know a thousand people, have been everywhere, done things. You could keep their guests entertained single-handed with nothing more than the story of one year out of your life. If they invited me, it was purely put of politeness and only for a visit. You, they'd want permanently."

She tried to speak, but he rushed on. "And if you refused their offer out of some kind of misguided loyalty to me, then call them back and say you've changed your mind."

She felt tears sting her eyes and blinked, refusing to shed them. "Rolph, will you pay attention to what I'm saying? I haven't changed my mind. I won't change my mind! I'm staying here, because here, with you, is where I want to be, and it's not out of any kind of misguided loyalty. I love you, Rolph. Why can't you believe that?"

With a groan, he reached out and linked his hands behind her neck. "I do," he said. "Sweetheart, I do believe you, but I know, so much better than you do, that it's not enough, that your wanderlust will win in the end."

She pushed his hands away and strode angrily to the other side of the office. "What do you mean," she asked, turning to face him, "you know so much better than I do? Rolph, it infuriates me when you make dumb statements like that. Look at me! Am I a child? Am I still that butterfly-brain you thought you were hiring out of friendship, or have you figured out yet that I am a grown woman with several grains of intelligence?"

He looked at her standing there, the sun in her flame-colored hair, her eyes filled with anger and sadness and confusion. "I know you're not a child," he said, his voice thick. Lord, after what they'd shared in the past week and a half, there was no way he could ever think of her as a child again. She was a woman, his woman. But for how long? That question always rose to plague him no matter how hard he tried to believe she meant what she said.

"I don't think of you as a child any longer," he went on. "What I'm saying is that I know from past personal experience that people who want to wander will wander, regardless of what they have to leave behind, regardless of whom it hurts. And as I told you before, I don't want to suffer that kind of hurt ever again." He stared at her for a moment, then added, "And I won't."

"Rolph! Wait!" she cried as he walked out of the office as if the conversation were over.

"What does that mean?" she asked, following him into his apartment. "You talk to me, Rolph McKenzie! I've had it with men who won't put into a relationship all they expect a woman to! This time, I'm not going to take it. We're both involved in this love affair and we're both damned well going to work at keeping it on track. So don't think you can shut me out and walk away like that, force me to make all the concessions, do all the adjusting. If I have to give up being completely independent, you've got to give up closing me out whenever you feel threatened. So talk. What did that statement mean? Did you have a prior relationship you haven't told me about? One important enough that you 'suffered,' that you were badly hurt?"

He looked at her stormily for several seconds, then wheeled and strode into the kitchen. "What I meant," he said, glaring back at her as she followed right on his heels, "is that I can't spend my adult life the way I did my childhood, waiting for someone I—" He stopped and set two glasses down hard on the counter. "Waiting for someone to come back from some jaunt I can't go on because I have responsibilities I won't ignore." He opened the ice compartment and grabbed a handful of cubes, flung them into the glasses, and then added a large splash of whiskey to each. He shoved one toward her and lifted the other, taking a hefty swallow before speaking again. "I told you. I want a home. I want a family. And I want my children to have a mother whose eyes don't light up at the thought of a different shore, a strange country, and another, and then another damned trip away!"

He ran a hand through his hair and sat on one of the two chairs, leaning his elbows on the table and propping his forehead on the heels of his hands. "Oh, hell, is it too much to ask that my kids be given a happier childhood than I had?"

"What?" Slowly, Marian walked over to him

and placed her hands on his shoulders, massaging his taut muscles. "Rolph? Were you unhappy as a child?" It was almost more than she could believe.

"No, of course not," he said, then lifted his head and turned to look at her bleakly. For several moments he didn't say anything. Then he burst out, "Oh, what the hell! Yes! Yes, dammit, I was unhappy as a child. I was miserable."

Nine

As he said the words aloud for the first time in his life, Rolph recognized their truth. He had always resented his parents' peripatetic life-style, even though they'd left him and Max in the kind and loving care of Freda Coin. And while he'd shared the resentment equally between his marine biologist mother and his civil engineer father, it was always his mother he missed the most.

The childhood pique had long since faded, but the deep need for stability in his life remained. He chewed on his lower lip, then dropped his gaze. Was that what it had all been about, he wondered, this search for his "ideal" woman? Yes. Of course. Somebody completely unlike his mother.

"I've never admitted that before," he said. "Not even to myself. All I ever knew was that I wanted something . . . someone really special, all mine, someone I wouldn't have to share, someone who'd always be there for me, but I never once thought that it might be because I was so unhappy as a kid. Until now."

"But why?" Marian asked. "Why were you unhappy? I don't understand. You had it all!"

Marian wanted to weep. He was tearing down the very foundation of *her* childhood beliefs! "You and Max," she said, "were everything I ever wanted to be. You were important to your parents, loved by them, popular with your friends because your home was such a fun place to visit. Not only that, you had each other. I envied you and Max so very much for the warm, close, happy family life you had, and it never occurred to me that you weren't the happiest, most secure children ever born."

He stood, flinging his hands out as he said, "With our parents away half the time? How could we have had a happy, secure childhood? Maybe by the time you were old enough to recognize different family types and found your own lacking, I'd learned to hide what I felt. But I hated never having a mom to come to school with cookies for the class party, never having my dad available when the Scouts had a father and son affair. And when my friends' fathers were teaching them to drive, mine was on a job in South America. You think that didn't bother me?"

She gripped her cold glass in both hands. "But—but surely there were compensations!" she protested. "I remember those exotic vacations you and Max used to get, trips to whatever foreign place your parents happened to be when summer vacation started, or Christmas holidays, or spring break. You'd come back tanned and handsome and full of stories of what you'd seen and done. I used to sit enthralled for hours and listen to you entertain your friends, the ones who had ordinary families and had to stay home. I know you enjoyed those trips, Rolph. You couldn't have made all that up." It was almost as if she were pleading with him to say he hadn't been different from what she'd always believed.

"No," he said, his anger subsiding so suddenly, it was as if it had never been. All that remained was sadness. "We didn't make anything up. We did have some wonderful times, but those trips never fully compensated me for what I really wanted—our parents, home, with us."

"Oh, Rolph . . ."

He led Marian into the living room and sat with her on the sofa, which, true to his promise, he'd bought. She set her drink on a new end table and faced him.

"Does Max feel this way?" she asked.

"Max? Hell, no. He's always been the tough one, the one who took everything life dished out and went looking for more. I tried to be like him, but long ago I knew I wasn't making it."

"I'd rather have you be you, than try to be Max," she said, then asked, "Did they know? Your parents?"

"Probably not. No. How could they have known how much their going away bothered me when I didn't even realize it myself until right now? Don't think I blame them for it," he added. "I know they did what they had to do, and were home as often as they could be. In a way, they were like your parents, though, loving each other so much, they tended to exclude us. Maybe that's why something in me responded to the solitary little kid you were. My parents didn't often both need to be away at the same time. They chose to be because they couldn't bear to be apart."

Marian nodded slowly. "I didn't realize that, but now that you say it I can see it must be true. After all, what could a marine biologist be doing to further her career in a road construction camp in the Andes?"

"Exactly. And while she was collecting and studying bivalve mollusks, it wasn't as though Dad was building anything more exciting than sand castles on a beach."

"You had Freda, at least." She had also envied the McKenzies their wonderfully funny housekeeper, who always had a hug and an extra cookie for the lonely little girl next door.

He smiled. "Oh, yes. And we adored her. Still do. But she wasn't our mother and it wasn't the same."

He cupped Marian's face in his hands and stared earnestly into her eyes. "So you see, when I saw you get so excited about the prospect of a cruise aboard *Catriona*, I remembered the way my mother looked every time Dad came home and said the company had a new contract, or when she got a grant from the university to go and research another text. She greeted news like that with the same eagerness as you did Slim and Ethel's invitation, and that was when I realized there wasn't much hope for us."

Tears flooded her eyes and spilled over. She paid them no heed. "There is," she said, wrapping her fingers around his wrists. "Please, believe me and trust me. That excitement was over the thought of both of us going on a cruise aboard *Catriona*, not me alone."

He kissed her gently. "But, baby, don't you see? Haven't you been listening? I don't want that kind of life. I simply don't share your wanderlust."

"You do! You must! You're the one planning a long honeymoon aboard *Sunrise VII*. If you didn't have any wanderlust, you'd plan something else, like a week at Club Med and then back to your roses and picket fence."

He let her go, smiling crookedly, and wiped her tears from her face. "That was a dream," he said.

"Sure! Like your perfect woman." She stood up. "Well, maybe it's time you stopped dreaming, Rolph, and looked at reality for a change. I'm going home. Good night. I'll see you tomorrow."

"No," he said, standing up too. "Don't leave, Marian. Stay with me, please." He slipped his arms around her, tilted her head back, and kissed her. "I'm sorry I got upset about that phone call. I only wish I could forget all the different places you've been, and how short a time you stayed in each one."

She drew a deep breath and stepped out of his arms. Picking up her untouched drink, she sipped the whiskey as she sank back down into the soft couch. "Rolph, maybe I should tell you about my wanderings, and why I moved on so often."

He sat again, looking wary. "Only if you want to."

"I think I have to." She smiled and touched his arm, running her fingernails over his shirt cuff with a light, rasping sound. She watched her own movement, not looking at him. "Oh, damn, this is going to sound so conceited!"

"Sweetheart, you're the least conceited person I know. Go ahead and tell me."

She couldn't meet his eyes, but turned her gaze to her drink, watching the little ripples in the glass. "In nearly every job I've had, there's been a man—and sometimes more than one—who made life . . . difficult for me."

"Difficult?"

She glanced up and saw confusion in his eyes. "They thought they'd hired my body, not my brain or my hands. They thought dispensing sexual favors was part of my job description. I don't know how other women handle it, but what I did was quit. After what Wendell had done to me, I wouldn't permit myself to be treated that way again. So I turned down invitations, slapped roving hands, made it clear that sex wasn't on the agenda, and if my boss thought it was, I'd move on." She drew in a deep breath. "I moved on often."

Rolph was thoughtful and silent for several minutes. One day, he wondered, would she include her job with him in these memories of hers? No! He immediately rejected the idea. If she hadn't wanted his sexual advances, she'd have quit. She was still there. Therefore, she welcomed them, just as she had told him that day aboard the boat. But what if they become unwelcome? If she tired of him? If something, somewhere, looked more attractive? What then?

"Every job?" he asked.

She looked up at him. "I said 'nearly' every job. There were times I quit for other reasons, like the boutique I started when I moved back here more than a year ago. It was a challenge getting it up and running, but then when Mom was so ill and the boutique was already holding its own, I sold it at a profit and devoted my time to taking care of Mom. I did run into a lot of harassment, though. Maybe most women know how to handle it better than I do. I simply couldn't stand it."

"Is that why you changed schools so often, too?"

"No. I know it can happen there, of course. Women are told that if they want passing grades, they have to put out for the professor. Luckily, I never had to worry about grades." She shrugged self-consciously. "That's one of the reasons I moved from school to school. I completed most of my courses in half the time allotted, then very often there was nothing more for me to do at that school until the following semester, sometimes even the following year. So I'd find another school offering something I wanted to take."

"Like six languages, a bachelor's degree in sociology, and an MBA."

She glanced at him again and sipped her drink. "Yes." She shrugged one shoulder, and he knew she was uncomfortable with the subject. "It's not that I work really hard, you see, it's simply that I find it very easy to learn."

He shook his head, smiling at her. "You're phenomenal, you know that? No wonder you're so damned easy to teach."

"Am I?" If she was, why couldn't he teach her to be what he wanted a woman to be, dependent, clinging, seeking protection?

He walked around behind the sofa and began massaging her shoulders. "I've told you before that you are. Remember?"

She smiled, recalling that day. "As I remember

it, you said 'touch,' not teach, then looked as if somebody was going to string you up for the error."

"That's how I felt. Every time I gave into my impulse to touch you, I could feel Max's eyes on me, and hear the lecture I got that day he found me teaching you to dance in our living room."

She shook his hands off and turned, surprised. "When I was sixteen? I don't remember his being there that day."

Rolph closed his eyes, gripping the back of the couch. "He was there. I'll never forget that day."

Marian cringed and buried her face against her knees. "Neither will I. The shame of it lived in me for years. Oh, Lord, I was so embarrassed."

He strode back around the sofa and sat beside her, urging her head up. For heaven's sake, he thought. She was blushing bright red. "You were embarrassed? Why?"

"Because I threw myself at you. There I was plastering myself against you, panting and drooling, all caught up in my first sexual arousal, and I didn't even know I was embarrassing you until I happened to look up and saw you all red in the face, gulping and sweating and . . . Yes, yes, I remember now, Max in the doorway. That was when I ran out of there like the hounds of hell were on my tail."

"And that, my sweet, was when Max turned into a hound from hell and nearly tore me apart. He forcibly reminded me that you were sixteen years old, a child, and I was twenty-four, and both our families trusted me to look after you properly. I was gulping and sweating and red in the face because I was within an inch of flinging you down on the sofa and ravishing your virginal little body, and Max saw that. There was utterly no doubt as to my condition."

She looked stunned for several seconds, then smiled radiantly. "You mean it wasn't just me who got turned on by our dances?"

"Hell, no! Lord, the insane fantasies I had after that. I couldn't bear to be in the same room as you. Never have I looked forward to anything more than I did the day you were due back at school. But even then the fantasies didn't stop."

"Hmm," she said. "I've always heard it's good for a couple to act out their fantasies. And here we are in a living room, with a sofa close at hand. Shall we dance, Mr. McKenzie?"

It was a very short dance.

Marian didn't realize until several days later that they never had resolved all of Rolph's fears and doubts. They'd allowed themselves to be sidetracked, and he still wasn't convinced she was content to stay. Events at her father's birthday party confirmed that.

"You," Jeanie said, turning Marian to the light streaming through a pair of tall French doors, "have a very distinctive glow about you, and I don't believe it has anything to do with the sunset." Her gaze flicked over toward Rolph where he stood with his and Marian's fathers at the other side of the room. "How goes the new job?" With a sly grin, Jeanie added, "And the new boss?"

Damn! Marian thought. Jeanie was the fifth person to mention that "glow." It was becoming increasingly difficult to pretend there was no reason for it beyond good health. She dug up a smile from somewhere and shrugged. "Rolph

and I work well together. I think he's finally
come to the conclusion that I do have a brain in
my head. I really enjoy what I'm doing there,
Jeanie. Thanks for moving me that direction."

She broke off as Max walked toward them,
guiding his small son in front of him while
Christopher practiced walking, clinging to his
father's index fingers. He wasn't quite confident
enough yet to go it alone. He beamed at Marian
as she crouched before him, then let go long
enough to launch himself at her. She caught
him, picked him up, and spun him around.

"Hi, there, little guy," she said, laughing into
his laughing face. "How you doing? Growing?
Getting fat?" She poked his tummy and he
giggled loudly, then hugged her neck.

She hugged him back. Lord, how she wanted
a baby! The feeling washed over her, an uncontrollable deluge of need. It got worse every time
she saw little Christopher. Until he was born,
she hadn't suspected she had a biological clock,
let alone that it was ticking. She squeezed her
eyes shut as pain struck. As much as she
wanted a baby, she knew she didn't want one
unless Rolph were its father.

And until they sorted out their difficulties,
that wouldn't happen. She wasn't even fully
convinced he wanted it to happen. The shadow
of his ideal woman continued to drift periodi-
cally over her newfound happiness.

Christopher objected to her tight hug and
squirmed to be set free. He held out his arms
eagerly to his grandmother as Zinnie and Rolph
joined the group. "Hey, stay and play with me,"
Marian said to the baby. "You can see your
grandma any old time."

"Let me have him," Zinnie said with a smile,

lifting Christopher out of Marian's arms. "You mustn't be greedy, dear. After all, you only need get busy and create a few of your own."

"And what would she do with them if she had them, Mother?" Rolph asked. "Marian's a traveler. There's only one Freda Coin in the world, and I'm afraid the McKenzie clan has already spent her."

Zinnie raised her brows at her younger son's testy tone. "Is Marian planning on leaving again soon?"

Before Marian could speak on her own behalf, Rolph shrugged and said, "She's had an offer and her contract with me has only a few weeks left to run."

Marian's throat was so tight, she could scarcely force any words out. "No, Aunt Zinnie. I'm not planning to leave. Rolph seems to be forgetting, I turned down that offer. Excuse me, please."

She turned to Jeanie. "Let's take our wine out onto the terrace. Seems a shame to miss that wonderful sunset."

"Sure," Jeanie said. "It's not every day I have so many free and willing baby sitters."

The two women walked outside to a grouping of thickly padded chairs and lounges, shaded by a big, oval umbrella and shielded from the house by massive redwood planters filled with pink geraniums and white petunias.

"Did I tell you that Christopher has three new teeth and said 'Mama' very clearly yesterday?" Jeanie asked, pulling a deck chair close to the chaise Marian huddled on.

Marian shook her head. Tears threatened. She didn't dare say a word.

"I tell you," Jeanie went on, "that little guy is

doing so well, changing so much, growing up so rapidly, I think we're going to have to get him a little sister soon." Jeanie spent the next fifteen minutes talking nonstop about her son, her business, and her wonderful, incomparable husband. By the time she was talked out, Marian had herself back in hand.

With a shaky smile, she sipped her wine, then said, "Thanks, Jeanie. I needed a bit of time out."

"I could see that. Want to talk about it?"

Marian shrugged. "There's nothing to talk about."

"Hey, come on. You're unhappy. I'm not thick, Marian, and I guess I feel responsible, because when I got you that job with Rolph, I suspected you were well on the way to being in love with him."

Marian sighed. After setting her glass on the table, she swung her legs up onto the chaise and wrapped her arms around her knees. "All right, I love him."

Jeanie nodded. "And from what I've seen, he loves you. The look on his face when you were swinging Christopher around could have set the North Pole on fire."

Marian shook her head. "If he does, he's never said it. He's waiting for the right woman to come along, someone who's solid and settled and completely uninterested in going anywhere farther than the nearest supermarket."

"I can't really believe that. Just looking at the guy tells me he's nuts about you."

"Maybe that's the way he sees his attraction to me. As a kind of craziness he'll get over. He . . . well, he admits he wants me." She shrugged, embarrassment barely at bay. She'd never had a girlfriend she could discuss intimate things with until Jeanie, and it didn't come easily to her. "I have to believe that. A guy can't hide it, can he?" She thought again of Wendell. There could be other reasons for passion, besides love.

Jeanie laughed and patted Marian's linked hands. "Not hardly. Maybe he's like his brother, afraid to use the 'L' word. Damn, what a stubborn crew the McKenzies are. Max is as bad as his brother. The trouble I had convincing that man he loved me!"

"Really? I thought the two of you came out of that cavern completely committed to each other."

"Oh, I'm not saying Max was reluctant to marry me, which is just as well, considering the shotgun I was carrying and didn't know it. He just didn't want to trust love." Jeanie frowned. "And I didn't want to trust marriage. I could only see my sister's first one as an example and I'd sworn it off."

She looked hard at Marian. "Maybe that's Rolph's problem, lack of trust. So how are we going to get him to trust you enough to see that you are his dream woman?"

"If I thought you had the answer, Jeanie, I'd make you sit here until you gave it to me."

"The answer to what?"

Marian started at Rolph's voice and swung her feet to the ground, smoothing the full skirt of her pale yellow sundress over her knees.

"That was rude, little brother," Max said. He lifted Jeanie out of her deck chair and seated himself in it, then set her on his lap. "We interrupted girl-talk. When doing that, a guy is not supposed to ask questions."

"Right," Rolph said. "I see I don't know as much about girls as you do."

He sat beside Marian, curling an arm around her and pulling her against his side. "But I'm trying to learn." She stiffened, sending him an uneasy glance.

"It's okay," he said. "Max knows about us." He grinned at her. "And I assume that 'girl-talk' included the subject of relationships in general, yours and mine in particular."

She gave him a weak smile. He didn't seem to mind Max and Jeanie knowing. Why, then, had he turned thundercloud-dark when his mother laughingly commented on their arriving together, and snapped at her when she mentioned Marian's becoming a mother? "It . . . came up," she admitted.

"We were sent to tell you two that dinner will be ready in ten minutes," Max said. Jeanie lithely sprang to her feet as he got up. "Don't be late," he admonished, and walked away with Jeanie tucked securely under his arm.

Rolph continued to sit. "Are you angry?"

Marian shook her head. "Of course not."

"I know we agreed to keep this private from our families, but Max guessed."

She looked at him. "Everyone's guessed, Rolph."

"I suppose so." He didn't seem happy about it. "But as long as they're only guessing, as long as we don't confirm anything, it won't matter so much when . . ."

Her brows drew together in a frown. "When it's over?"

"I don't want it to be over," he said, pulling her into a tight, almost desperate embrace.

"Neither do I!"

As they clung together, Marian felt as if they were on the edge of a crumbling precipice, and the least little movement from either would send them into an abyss. She wanted something solid, something real, something more tangible than mutual desire to strengthen their relationship, give it substance.

Trust would do, she thought, and pulled herself reluctantly from his embrace. Trust. Nothing more, nothing less. Why was it too much to ask for?

"Marian? Honey?" Rolph bent over the bed and kissed her. It was just daybreak.

"I don't want to get up," she grumbled, pulling the pillow over her head. "It's too early."

"I know. You don't have to get up now. I only wanted to tell you that I'm going."

She sat up to find him sitting on the side of the bed, fully dressed. She yawned and leaned on him. "I'll miss you," she said. "Call me every night?"

"I promise," he said, and kissed her before laying her back down. He closed his eyes for a moment, then looked at her again, drawing the sheet off her body. "Talk about fantasies," he said, bending to kiss one upstanding nipple. "There's something in every man that gets turned on by the idea of his woman lying naked and waiting for him, while he's fully clothed."

She shoved him away and pulled the sheet over her. "It must be one of those male power things, on a par with wanting her barefoot and pregnant. It's not one of my fantasies, nor have I run into it as one in any women's book I've ever read."

He grinned. "Now that you mention it, neither have I."

They shared a smile and a deep, longing kiss, then he was gone.

Rolph called that night and every night from San Francisco, but the calls weren't an adequate replacement for his presence. Marian hadn't known it was possible to miss someone so much, or for days to pass so slowly.

The night before he was to return, after their long talk, she fell into a restless sleep and dreamed of him. He was on a sailboard in her parents' swimming pool, careening off the side while she begged him to take it out to the bay where it belonged. He sailed on, telling her to try it, it was fun. She woke up in a sweat, wondering if the dream meant that he was right, that their goals in life were too disparate for them to have a future together. If she wasn't secretly longing for more space, why would the sight of him sailing in such a confined area have bothered her so badly? Would she, as time passed, become like his mother and be compelled to seek out far shores?

No, dammit, she wouldn't. She wasn't like that! She would always remember her own childhood experiences just as Rolph remembered his and was affected by them. If she had children, she'd love them to distraction. They'd probably grow up warped, she'd smother them so much rather than risk their feeling left out.

But . . . had Aunt Zinnie believed, too, that nothing would ever pull her away from her children?

There was no answer to be had in the dark,

and eventually Marian fell asleep again, only to waken to the shrill sound of the phone.

"Hi, Ms. Crane," a young male voice replied to her slightly panicky hello. "This is Brewster, down at the marina. I hate to disturb you, especially on a night like this, but with Mr. McKenzie away I didn't know what else to do."

As the boy spoke, Marian became aware of rain driving noisily against her window, pushed by a high wind. "You were right to call me if there's a problem, Brewster. What's up?"

"You know the boat that guy put on the rocks a couple of days back, *Calico Cat*? Well, with this storm it's kinda bumpy even in here behind the breakwater tonight, and the patch must have broke loose on his hull. That sucker's going down. He got so low in the water his batteries cut out so his own pumps aren't working, and when I tried to hook up the dockside pump, I found it's on the fritz too. We're gonna lose that boat!"

Marian thought fast, picturing the position of the damaged boat in the marina. "Okay, Brewster, I'm on my way. Meanwhile, you get *Sunrise VII* moved over and rafted up to her starboard side. Tie them tightly together, Brewster. Then sling ropes from the wharf under both boats at bow and stern and fasten them securely to *Sunrise VII*'s starboard rail. Got that? Her starboard side. Otherwise she'll roll with the weight of *Calico Cat* and they'll both go down. I'll call Southland Marina and ask for a spare pump." She didn't wait for Brewster's response, and was already peeling her nightshirt off over her head as she hung up the phone.

There was little traffic at three-thirty in the morning, but the streets were slick with rain.

Still, Marian arrived at the marina in minutes and found several people milling around the wharf beside *Calico Cat*, a forty-five foot cruiser listing badly even with Rolph's sailboat tied alongside to provide buoyancy. The neighboring marina had brought its pump and put it into operation, and Marian made her way through the crowd of onlookers to thank the men who had brought it.

She turned back to Brewster, wiping rain from her eyes. "Has her owner been contacted?"

The boy shook his head. "There's no answer at his house. One of the other boat owners said something about a golf tournament, but he doesn't remember where."

"Then I'll have to make arrangements to get her out of the water at once. I'll be in the office on the phone if you need me. As soon as she's pumped dry enough to be moved, she'll have to go to dry dock."

The rain had eased to a fine drizzle by the time *Calico Cat* was finally stabilized and pumped as dry as possible. Her patch was repaired by a diver who arrived at daybreak, then she was towed to a boat yard several miles away where she would be put up on blocks to await her owner's instructions.

Drained of energy, Marian sat slumped at her desk and stared blindly at their standard marina contract, wondering if what she had done was going to cost the marina a punishing amount of money. And, oh Lord, what would Rolph have to say about the actions she'd taken? Again, because it was her way, she'd acted on her own, just as she had the day her car was stolen. Would he say she should have called him in San Francisco before ordering that boat hauled out? Had she taken too much on herself? It hadn't even occurred to her until now that maybe she shouldn't have taken over that way, made arbitrary decisions. Was she ever going to learn to be a team player, half of a partnership?

She searched the contract again, trying to make sense of the legal jargon, but she was too tired to concentrate. With a sigh, she leaned on the desk, pillowing her head on her arms, still shivering in spite of a hot shower and dry clothes. She'd rest for a few minutes, then go over the confusing legalese again until she found something to justify her impulsive actions. . . .

She was sliding down a long chute from a light doze toward a deep sleep, when a touch on her shoulder brought her jerking upright. She blinked to clear her eyes, then blinked again because she couldn't believe what they told her.

"Rolph!" At once, she felt better, love and relief flowing through in her in such vast proportions, for a moment she couldn't begin to form another word. "Rolph . . ." Her voice cracked. "Oh, I'm so glad you're home. We almost lost a boat last night and I couldn't reach the owner so I had it put in dry dock and now I can't find anything in the contract that authorizes us to do that and—"

"I've heard all about it, and you are going to bed," he said, lifting her out of her chair and heading for his apartment with her in his arms. "You're exhausted."

"No. No, I'm fine." She struggled, but he held her firmly. "I can do my job, Rolph. I'm not some little flower who's going to wilt over lack of sleep."

"I know that, but anybody who's been up half the night rescuing some idiot's boat deserves at least the morning off." He set her down on his bed and tossed her a T-shirt from his open suitcase. "Get into that and into bed."

She sat looking at him, seeing the concern in his eyes, the desire, and something else besides. It made her heart swell and take flight. He touched her hair with one hand, lightly. "You know what?" he said.

She ached with weariness, and with wanting him. She shook her head. "No. What?"

"I know I did one thing right."

"What's that?"

"When I took you on as my assistant, I hired the 'right man' for the job."

"I feel like a little girl," Marian said, smiling at Rolph, who had come in to wake her. It was nearly six in the evening and she was horrified to have slept the entire day. She hugged a stuffed toy seal to her breast. It had soft gray fur and huge, pitiful eyes.

"You don't look like a little girl," Rolph said. He sat on the bed and leaned toward her to hang a gold nugget on a chain around her neck.

She lifted it and stared at it. "Wow! This would have kept a forty-niner in luxury for a lifetime."

"I remember your saying that to get the gold, you sometimes have to dig through an awful lot of dirt." He kissed her. "I want you to have the gold, honey, and never have to dig through dirt to get it."

"Thank you." Even more than the gift delighted her, she was pleased and touched that he remembered what she'd said about finding the gold in life. She ran a hand through his thick hair. "I've found all the gold I want."

He opened a box and popped a piece of chocolate into her mouth. "Now, it seems to me that a century or two ago, before I went away, I was having a hell of a good fantasy about you in this bed, and I don't want my acting it out interrupted by you suddenly saying you're starving to death."

She swallowed her chocolate. "If you mean the fantasy with you fully dressed and me fully naked, then I don't like it."

He grinned. "No? And what would make you like it?"

She stripped her T-shirt off over her head and growled. "Get out of that suit, McKenzie. Now!"

Laughing, he did so.

Ten

Later, idly twisting one of her curls around his index finger, Rolph said, "I did a lot of thinking while I was away. I'm beginning to have a better understanding of my parents. I don't think I'm going to be able to go away without you again. That was the longest week in my life."

She searched his face in the dim light cast by the security lamp on the dock below. "The understanding doesn't make you happy, does it?"

Slowly, he shook his head. "Not really. It means that I'm going to have to reassess a lot of concepts I thought were firm in my mind. Beliefs about myself, about my vision of right and wrong. It'll mean compromising some of my ideals, I guess."

Marian sat up and turned on the light to see him better. "Seeking compromise isn't exactly a new concept, Rolph. People have been doing it for centuries to make their relationships work." She smiled and tapped his chin with one finger.

"Only, by tradition, it was the woman who had to make all the adjustments and changes."

"Yes." He frowned, and she traced the wrinkled line of his brow. "But women aren't so willing to do that anymore, are they?"

"Some are, some aren't. Maybe it depends on how badly they want the relationship, and how badly they want the things they'll be forced to compromise for."

Suddenly, Rolph wanted to know how much Marian would be willing to compromise, but he knew the only way to find out was to ask her. His heart hammered hard in his chest. *Ask her to marry you, you coward,* he told himself. *Go ahead and do it!*

So far, all their discussions had been academic, because they were talking about "what if" situations. Only by declaring himself would he have the right to know what concessions she'd make, have the right to negotiate, make demands on her. He swallowed hard, trying to form words, but his mouth was so dry he couldn't speak. He could only look at her beautiful face as doubts washed over him in waves.

So, instead of speaking, he dragged her into his arms and kissed her until there was no possibility of talk. All the while he silently said the words he couldn't make himself say aloud. *I love you, I love you, I love you. . . . Be mine.*

"Victory!" Marian strode into the office several days later, filled with elation. "Jefferson McQuade has just signed a purchase agreement for *Stephanie-Jayne*, and a contract to moor her here in one of the boathouses, berth E-12, for at least the next year. I'm going to change, then go help him bring her over from Ambrose Bay."

"Good for you," Rolph said. "You certainly have a knack for selling, and an intuitive ability to match the right boat with the right owner."

Marian glowed at his praise, and he followed her as she walked into his apartment, where she kept boating clothes for times such as this. Watching her slip out of her skirt and into a pair of jeans, he thought of how much he loved to look at her, especially when she'd been out in the fresh air and wind. It made her cheeks glow and her eyes shine, and tossed her glorious hair into an abandoned tangle that reminded him of the way she looked in the morning. Marian was not an indoor person. She needed the wind and the sea and the brightness of sunshine. She needed space, freedom to fly. . . .

He clamped down on that thought. It wasn't something he wanted to dwell on. She was right, he had to trust her, believe in her, and he did. Ever since they'd talked and he'd explained to her—and to himself—how his childhood still affected his outlook on life, he'd known that he was wrong to blame Marian for something that hadn't been her doing; wrong to believe that because his mother hadn't stayed with him, Marian would leave him too. If, at moments like these, he had the odd doubt, that was something he'd have to deal with. It wasn't as if he doubted her love.

"What was the final selling price?" he asked.

"Two-fifty," she said from inside a sweatshirt. Her tousled head appeared as she continued. "Mrs. Alderling wanted two-seventy-five, but she knew she was being unrealistic and was willing to come down after I had a quiet talk with her."

Rolph raised one brow as he shouldered himself up from his slumped position against the bedroom door. "I had several 'quiet' talks with the widow Alderling about her unrealistic idea of the value of *Stephanie-Jayne*. She made me feel I was trying to cheat an old lady. How come you succeeded where I failed?"

Marian gave him a wide-eyed, innocent look as she sat on the edge of his bed and stuffed her feet into deck shoes. "Just smarter, I guess." She cocked her head sideways. "Want some lessons?"

He checked to see that the door leading to his apartment was closed, then stalked across the room to her. He pulled her to her feet and held her close. "Yeah," he said. "What have you got to teach me today?"

Long moments later, he lifted his head. "I'll come with you and help you move that boat around." He wanted to be with her, even though the agony of seeing her, touching her, and still having to wait for the workday to be finished before he could make love to her properly nearly killed him.

She smiled. "Thanks. Jefferson McQuade is a pain in the . . . left heel. He knows little about boats except that he wants one. And now that he has one, he also wants me to give him lessons on handling it."

"I hope you told him to get lost."

"I told him to join the Power Squadron."

As they walked through the outer office, Kaitlin held up a hand. "Just a sec, Rolph. Somebody wants to talk to you."

"Sorry," he said, grabbing Marian's hand and heading for the door. "Take a message. I'll be out for the rest of the afternoon."

"But . . ."

"Kaitlin. A message."

"Yes, sir."

"I can do this alone," Marian said, holding the door closed so he couldn't open it. "Go and take that call. It might be important."

"Nothing's more important to me than being with you," he said. "Now, let's go. We mustn't keep your client waiting."

Marian heard the edge in his voice. He wouldn't be acting this way if her client were just a nice old lady putting her late husband's boat on the market. It was only now that the nice old lady was out of the picture he was getting all het up. "Rolph," she said softly, "He's my client and I can deal with him. That person on the phone is your client. How can you keep him—or her—waiting?"

He glowered at her for a moment, then nodded. "All right, all right. Sometimes I wonder who's the businessman here, you or me. Seems you've got a better handle on things than I have most of the time."

Marian remembered that statement later in the week when, on the verge of leaving for the day, she met a young couple with three little children in tow striding eagerly up the ramp toward the office.

"Hello," the man said. "I'm Garry Anderson and this is my wife, Tina. Is Mr. McKenzie here? We managed to get away a day early and we'd like to get the papers signed right now, if possible, so we could sleep aboard and not have to pay for a hotel."

"I'm sorry," she said. "He isn't here and I don't think I can reach him." Rolph had gone with Max to help him fly in a fresh load of fuel for the furnace in Max's mountain cottage. They wouldn't be back until morning.

"Maybe I could help?" she went on. "I'm his assistant and work closely with him on many of his sales."

"Maybe you can," Garry said. He looked, she thought, like a young golden lab, all legs and ears and wriggling glee.

"Then come in and we'll talk."

She got paper and colored pencils for the children to draw with, seated the Andersons in the reception area, then made a fresh pot of coffee while Garry and Tina burbled on excitedly about their first purchase of a sailboat. They'd never been sailing, either of them, but loved to watch the boats out the kitchen window of their house up-island and pretend they owned one. When Tina's grandmother died and left them some money, they decided to put it to use making their daydream a reality.

"Then we read about the *Condor* in a boating magazine," Garry continued, "and saw that Mr. McKenzie was handling it. We phoned him right away."

"*Condor*?" Marian turned from the coffee machine and gaped at Garry Anderson. "Jake Lehar's boat?"

"Yeah, that's the guy who's selling it. Why? Is something wrong, Ms. Crane?"

She blew out a long stream of air. "Yes, I'm afraid there is."

It took her nearly an hour and several refills of coffee before she made the young couple see just what was wrong, and another half hour of going through listings with them before she thought she had found the right boat for their needs.

"Gee, thanks, Ms. Crane," Tina said, holding

two of her children by their hands as they prepared to leave. "We owe you one. We'll call Mr. Lehar and tell him we've changed our minds."

"No, you don't have to do that. Rolph or I will take care of it."

"Oh, but he's expecting us," Garry explained. "We let him know we were coming down today and would want the key tonight. But now we won't, of course, so it's only polite to let him know. We like to do the right thing," he added. "It sets a good example for the kids."

I like to do the right thing too, Marian thought as she drove home, feeling good about what she had done. Part of matching the right boat with the right buyer was making sure the buyer didn't get the wrong one. Only this time, it hadn't been instinct working for her, but direct and personal knowledge of the boat. Lord, what a disaster it would have been if those kids had bought *Condor.* She couldn't understand where Rolph's mind had been when he made that deal. She smiled, hoping it had been on her.

Rolph hung up the phone and turned to face Marian as she walked into the office the next morning.

"My God!" he said, getting to his feet slowly as if his body weighed three times what it should. "What have you done?"

"I don't know," she said, setting her shoulder bag on her desk while fixing her gaze on his white face. She could see he was livid. Never had she seen Rolph so angry about anything. "What have I done?"

"What you've done," he said through clenched teeth, "is ruined a perfectly fine deal, one I initiated, one I intended to see through. I come back after one lousy day away to find that you've screwed it up because of some ancient personal grudge you have with the vendor? Dammit, I thought better of you! I trusted you! What I want to know is why, for God's sake, did you do it?"

"It appears," she said, her own temper held under tight control, "that you already have all the answers. Why ask me? I assume that was Jake Lehar on the phone?"

"Yes, that was Jake Lehar, and your knowing that without being told confirms his story. Marian, for the love of heaven, where was your judgment? What were you thinking of? Dammit, we'll be bloody lucky to pull this one off now, but maybe if I work fast and talk fast, I can manage it. Where's the file?" He strode over to her desk, gathered up a stack of file folders, and riffled through them. "Good, here it is."

"No." Eyes alive with fire, she slapped the files back down onto her desk, holding them there with both hands. "No, Rolph. Dammit!" she exclaimed as he wheeled back to his own desk and flipped through his Rolodex. "Listen to me!"

Still clutching the files, Marian raced across the room and grabbed the phone from Rolph. "Who are you calling?"

"The Andersons, of course."

"No," she said again, vehemently. "You can't sell those kids Lehar's boat! It would be murder."

He stared at her. "Murder? What are you talking about?"

"I'm talking about that death trap Lehar calls a boat."

"You're crazy, Marian. The stress of the job has gotten to you. Your thought-processes have

winged out. *Condor's* a perfectly sound boat."
He set her aside with little gentleness and grabbed the file she'd refused to give him. He pulled a page from it and shoved it under her nose. "Here. Read the surveyor's report and then tell me what's unsound about the boat, what makes it a death trap."

"I've read it," she said, shoving it aside. "I read it last night, and sure, it makes no mention of weak planks or rotted decks or crumbling superstructure. But no surveyor's report can tell the full story. Clearly, Jake Lehar didn't tell it either."

"Dammit, I know Jake Lehar. He's a good friend of mine. If there was something wrong with that boat, he'd know about it."

"If he wants to sell it badly enough, he wouldn't tell you about it."

"Of course he would. Jake's an honorable man. I've done business with him before. I've played golf with him, cards. He doesn't cheat."

"Maybe not, but he lies, Rolph. He lies by omission. Now, do you want to hear why I made the decision I made, or do you want me to walk out of here?"

"Marian! Now, just one damn minute here. Aren't you getting a little bit carried away? We're having a disagreement, sure, but that doesn't mean you have to walk out. I know you don't like Jake, but it's wrong to let that color your judgment in a business deal, a deal I made and intend to see stand, regardless of your opinion."

"You're quite right I don't like Lehar, but that has nothing to do with my professional judgment, which tells me it would be tantamount to murder to sell his boat to a pair of utter novices like the Andersons."

"Your 'professional' judgment is wrong, Marian. Be . . . adult enough to admit it."

She narrowed her eyes. "Why do I get the feeling you almost said 'man' enough to admit it?" she demanded. "What happened to my being the 'right man' for the job, Rolph? What happened to my 'intuitive' ability to match the right boat with the right owner? Have you forgotten about that so soon, or were you just pretending to believe in it because you like me in your bed? I don't take this kind of treatment from anybody, as Jake Lehar would tell you if he were capable of telling the truth! So fine, you go ahead and call the Andersons. Go ahead and sell them *Condor,* and when they capsize her and drown themselves and their three children in the first little blow they're out in, it can be on your conscience. I won't have it on mine."

"Marian, Marian, the surveyor's re—"

"I'm not talking about a piece of paper with a bunch of typing on it!" she shouted. "Or about figures and specs and provenance. I'm talking about Lehar's boat. It's a cow! It's cranky and unforgiving and no boat for people who have never sailed a day in their lives, not even as passengers. I know that boat, Rolph! I've sailed aboard her. I've seen her in action and believe me, she should have been scuttled the day she was launched, and Jake Lehar with her."

As she talked, she grabbed up personal items from her desk and jammed them into her shoulder bag. "But Lehar neglected to tell you that, didn't he? He forgot about the times the sailboat from hell went belly-up from trying to cross a ferry's wash, or turned turtle in a tiderip when the wind came across her port bow and she had a bit too much sail up for the conditions. And

I'm sure he just as conveniently forgot to tell you that he was the landlord last year for my boutique, and not only did he offer me lower rent in return for sexual favors, he made the same damned offer when he came to my apartment last night. Only this time he said if I treated him nice, he'd forget to mention to you that I'd told the Andersons to look elsewhere for their first boat."

Her desk top cleared, she whirled to face Rolph. "That's the kind of man your friend Jake Lehar is, Rolph. That's the man whose story you were willing to believe without even giving me a chance to defend myself. Well, no more. I'm gone. If you won't fire me, I quit."

"Marian!" He held his hands out to her. "I didn't know! I didn't even know the Andersons had never sailed before!"

"That's right, but you also didn't ask. You didn't give me the benefit of the doubt and that's what I can't forgive. You've never given me that, Rolph. You always assumed the worst of me, that since I moved from job to job, from school to school, from country to country, I was irresponsible and couldn't settle down. But that's not true. What I couldn't do was find a home that felt right to me. I thought I'd found it with you, but I was wrong. I've been wrong before, though, and gotten over it. I'll get over it this time too."

She picked up her little gray stuffed seal and tried to cram it into her bag. It wouldn't fit, so she set it back on her desk.

"Good-bye, Rolph," she said, then turned and walked to the door.

"Sure," he said. "Go ahead. Quit. It's nothing more than I expected of you."

She turned to face him. "I know. That's why I'm going. It's not because of this incident, Rolph. This was just the climax of all the other times you've called my judgment into question, decided without justification that I couldn't be telling the truth, that my promises weren't to be believed. That's not the kind of love I want. But I'm forgetting, aren't I? You never have said that you love me. You couldn't do that, could you, because you've never let yourself be sure enough of me."

He opened his mouth to tell her she was wrong, but before he could form even those simple words, she was gone. He sat at her desk, his head in his hands, then picked up the seal and flung it across the room. It hit the wall, bounced, and skidded into a corner where he let it lie.

Marian slammed the door to the office they had shared and marched out, looking neither left nor right. Head high, eyes straight ahead, down the ramp she strode, past *Sunrise VII*, through the marina, and up the ramp on the other side, to her car.

At her apartment she filled her suitcases, then took them downstairs and stowed them in the trunk of her car. She left the apartment key with a note and a check in the landlady's mailbox and drove to her parents' home.

"Marian!" Thea Crane said in surprise as her daughter entered the house. "My darling, what's happened to you? Are you ill?"

Her mother's startled exclamation was her undoing, and Marian shattered where she stood.

•   •   •

It took Rolph longer.

A day passed. A night. Another.

On the third morning he looked at his haggard image in the bathroom mirror and said to it, as he had the day before, and the day before that, "She's gone. You're here. You're alive. Shower, shave, dress. Keep going."

But that morning, something was different. He had no strength, not even the minimal energy it took to shower, shave, dress, and keep going. He shook his head, rubbed hand over his rough jaw, and went back into his bedroom. He didn't want to get dressed. He didn't want to keep going. He didn't want to do anything except think of Marian.

As he stared out his bedroom window, her face superimposed itself over the harbor, her eyes aglow with a pure, hot light as she said, her voice shaking with the strength of her emotion, *I love you, Rolph McKenzie.* He remembered how those words had filled his soul with joy, and how, on the verge of confessing his own love, he'd permitted doubts to surge up and silence him. So he'd taken the love exploding in his heart and used it to show her with his body the depth and breadth of his passion for her, his tenderness, his adoration.

Yet in the end, passion, adoration, and tenderness hadn't been enough, and he'd let her go. He'd stood there and watched her walk out the door. He hadn't run after her, hadn't begged her to stay.

Why?

"Because it was best for her," he said aloud. "Because, whether she would admit it or not, she wanted to go."

Bull, a voice in his head responded succinctly.

Rolph turned from the window. Yes, it was a load of manure, wasn't it? What was he doing, kidding himself like this? There was one reason and one reason only for his having let Marian walk away.

Slowly, he faced it, put it into words in his mind: *I didn't let her go because the tension of waiting for her to leave was too painful. I let her go because I was afraid to accept her love.*

"Oh, hell!" he groaned, pacing to the bathroom. He leaned on the sink again and stared into the mirror. "You total idiot! What in the name of all that's holy have you done!"

He tugged on a pair of jeans and a clean shirt, quickly ran a razor over his face, then brushed his teeth roughly. "And what are you going to do to make it better, bonehead?"

"Good morning, Rolph. How nice to see you." Thea Crane offered her papery cheek for a kiss. Rolph dutifully complied. "George and I are having breakfast on the terrace. Won't you join us?" Linking her arm through his, she led him across the tiled foyer to a pair of French doors. After ushering Rolph outside, she left him, murmuring something he didn't hear. He and George had just finished greeting each other and commenting on the long-lasting summer weather, when Thea returned with a fresh place setting and several crusty rolls in a basket.

"And Marian?" Rolph asked, standing quickly and pulling out a chair for his hostess. "Will she be joining us, or is she sleeping in?" He knew from Kaitlin, whom he'd sent around with her things from the office, that Marian had vacated her apartment the same day she walked out on him.

George passed Rolph the basket of rolls, looking surprised. "Marian's not here," he said. "Unless she came after I went to bed last night. Did she, dear?"

Thea shook her head as she filled a coffee cup for Rolph. "No." She smiled and offered Rolph the butter and a bowl of raspberry jelly. "She stopped in briefly a couple of days ago, but we haven't seen her since, or spoken to her."

He went colder inside. "But where is she?"

"I have no idea," Thea said.

Rolph halted in the act of tearing a roll in half. "Haven't you even heard from her?"

"No, but then, why should we? We don't live in each other's pockets, Rolph. Sometimes weeks go by without our being in touch, and it's only been a few days, after all."

"But she's moved out of her apartment! She wouldn't disappear without telling you where she was. Aren't you worried about her?" Rolph frowned. "She worries about you, you know," he added accusingly, feeling anger rise at their cavalier attitude. Dammit, Marian's parents had always been like this, completely indifferent to the needs of their only child.

"Marian? She worries about us?" George shook his head. "Why would she?"

"About Thea." Rolph swung his angry gaze toward his hostess. "Listen to me! One of the reasons she came to me for a job was so she'd be nearby in case you fell ill again, so I know she wouldn't have—"

"Oh, but it was months ago I was ill, dear," Thea interrupted with a laugh, patting Rolph's hand. "I'm fine now, honestly, so there's no need for Marian to stay close to home. She knows that."

Yes, there is a need, he wanted to say. *I'm the reason she should have stayed!*

"She's always been a free spirit," George said, spreading jelly on his roll.

"Well, if you're not concerned, I am," Rolph said. He shoved his chair back and stood. "She's been out of touch for too long. Can't you see it? That's not like her!"

"But, Rolph, of course it is," Thea said, standing also and taking his arm. "Come along now, sit down again. You haven't had a bite of breakfast. You mustn't let Marian's comings and goings upset you. And if you and she . . . well, if the two of you had something going, and she left you in the lurch, so to speak, then I can only say I'm sorry if you've been hurt. Marian's not always the most . . . reliable or thoughtful of girls. She's never stuck to anything or anyone for long. Tsk. That marriage of hers, remember?"

He hated hearing what could have been his own words thrown back at him. That assessment was, after all, nearly two months out of date. Didn't her own parents know that much about her? Hell, it was more out of date than that! Of course it had been longer than that since Marian had begun to act differently. It had simply taken them all too long to see it.

"You're wrong," he said, gently working his arm free from Thea's hold. "Maybe that's the way she used to be, but she's changed. Haven't you seen it, either of you? She didn't just up and go on a whim!" He closed his eyes and gripped the back of his chair for a moment before facing Marian's parents squarely. "She left because I hurt her and now I have to find her. I must see her, Thea. There are things I need to say to her. Help me."

"Rolph, I'm sorry, dear. We can't help you."

George stood and patted Rolph's shoulder. "If we hear from her, son, we'll be sure to tell her what you said."

He stared at them, not sure if he believed them. But why would they lie to him? Unless Marian had asked them to. "Yeah. Right. Thanks, and I'm sorry for interrupting your breakfast. I guess I'll go next door and see my family, since I'm out here anyway."

His parents weren't home, but Max, Jeanie, and Freda were just finishing their breakfast while Christopher staggered around the kitchen, caroming off walls and furniture. All three adults looked up as Rolph walked into the kitchen. None greeted him. Christopher bounced off his father's leg and into Rolph's.

Rolph scooped him up. "You're going to have to do better at getting around than that, buddy. You look like a hockey player. Or the puck."

"Coffee?" Freda asked, giving him a look that suggested she might put arsenic in it.

He ignored her sour expression. Obviously he'd transgressed, but would only learn how in Freda's time. "Black and strong and plentiful," he said, sitting in the chair his brother kicked away from the table for him. He bounced his nephew on his knee and stared at his brother and sister-in-law. Both stared back without any warmth he could detect.

Rolph suppressed a sigh. So they knew. And they blamed him. Well, why not? He blamed himself too. Yet, somehow, their silent censure made him ache just a little bit more. "All right," he said. "I see you know that Marian's gone. So I blew it. I want to fix it, dammit. Where is she? Her parents were as sweet as pie and lying through their teeth. They claim they don't know."

Max shrugged. "Then how should we?"

Rolph appealed to his sister-in-law. "Jeanie, you know, don't you?"

"Why do you care where she is?"

"Why do I care?" He watched Freda set his cup of coffee far enough away so that the baby couldn't reach it, and almost so far away that he couldn't reach it himself. "I care where she is because I made a big mistake and I want to make it better. If I can."

"What makes you so sure it was a mistake?" Max asked. All three adults focused their attention on Rolph. Sweat broke out on his brow. Was this what the Spanish Inquisition had felt like to a suspected heretic?

"It was a mistake because I let her go without telling her I love her. I let her go because I was angry. I believed she'd made a stupid business error out of spite and I took the other person's side instead of hers. I forgot everything I'd learned about her in the past two months, that she wasn't drifting through her job with me, putting in time until something else captured her attention. She'd come to learn, and she had learned. I forgot that she'd always done a good job, even when it meant getting out of bed in the middle of a cold, rainy night to make decisions about a sinking boat. She gave the job everything she had."

He drew in a deep breath and met Jeanie's

eyes, then tried to meet Max's and couldn't quite. "She gave *me* everything she had. And I didn't recognize it as permanent because it didn't come with a lot of pretty promises."

"And if you knew where she was now," Max asked, "would you go to her and still hope to get those promises?"

Rolph looked up, this time meeting his brother's gaze. "Yes," he said. "A guy can't stop hoping. But if what she can give me is herself without guarantees, then that's what I'll accept, because she's what I want."

Max stood, fished deep in his pocket, and pulled out a single key. Rolph recognized it at once as belonging to Max's 4x4, and suspected his brother had held it ready for this moment. Max bounced it on his hand for a moment, then tossed it to Rolph.

"Go for it," he said, and as Rolph caught the key, he knew where Marian was hiding.

He smiled and set his nephew on the floor to practice staggering some more. "Thanks," he said, and turned to leave.

"Wait!" Jeanie ran to him and gave him a swift, powerful hug. Then, slipping three of the six golden bangles she wore off her wrist, she handed them to Rolph.

"Give these to Marian, with my love."

Max shook his head. "Aw, Jeanie, for Pete's sake—" he began, but she cut him off with a sharp look.

"Never mind," she said. "You don't have to believe in Grandma Margaret's powers. I do. My sister Sharon does. And I think Marian will after today," she added, addressing, Rolph again. "When everything is right for two lovers, my Gypsy grandmother is happy, and she makes the bangles ring like chimes in the wind. Only a person with a Gypsy heart can hear them."

Rolph laughed, twirling the bangles around on one finger. Then he shrugged and dropped them into his shirt pocket. He was willing to try anything that might help him with Marian, and as a born wanderer, Marian must surely have a Gypsy heart.

As he had nearly two years ago when he'd driven Jeanie there to confront Max in his mountain retreat, Rolph parked the truck out of sight of the cabin. Not because he was afraid Marian might jump into a helicopter and fly away as Jeanie had feared Max would, but because he wanted to walk for a few minutes in order to calm himself, to get his thoughts together, to plan what he was going to say. Whatever it was, he knew, it was going to have to be good. He cast his mind back over all those romance novels he'd read, trying to remember the dialogue that had worked best under similar circumstances, when a guy had done wrong, had caused pain, and wanted to make amends.

There were so many different things he could say, so many different ways he could begin. Oh, Lord, he should have parked five miles away! He was never going to figure out what to say, or how to say it. Not in time.

In the end, when he stepped onto the covered porch and found Marian sitting in a chair, her feet on the railing, her nose in a book, he simply walked up to her, took the book away, pulled her to her feet, and said, "I love you. Please come home."

After that, it was easy.

• • •

Several hours later, Marian rolled over and sat up. It was dark in the loft bedroom and she struck a match, lighting the kerosene lamp on the bedside table. "Where do you think you're going?" Rolph asked, pulling her back down across his chest.

"I'm being unromantic again," she said. "I'm starving!"

He laughed. "When aren't you?" But he let her go. "What are you going to get?"

"Scrambled eggs," she said, picking up his shirt and shaking it out. Three fine golden hoops fell out of the pocket. Raising her brows, she retrieved them from the down comforter. "What are these for?"

He took them from her and twirled them on his finger again. "Jeanie sent them. She said something about her grandmother making music with them when everything was right between two lovers. Max pulled a face and rolled his eyes in that expression we intelligent males use when we're too smart to say 'Women!' out loud. What's it all about?"

Marian shrugged and pulled his shirt on. When she stood, it covered her nearly to her knees. "I haven't a clue." She set the bracelets on the bedside table. "You going to come and help me scramble eggs?"

He not only helped her scrambled eggs, he helped her clean up afterwards. "You have toast crumbs . . . here," he said, after they'd set their empty plates on the floor beside the bed. He bent to collect the crumbs with the tip of his tongue. "And here, and here, and . . . here."

"Mmm," Marian murmured, stretching languidly. "And what about here?"

"Maybe just one or two . . . Oh, look what I found."

"Rolph!" She squirmed. "My toast was nowhere near there!"

"Crumbs fall," he said, and continued his search. "We wouldn't want any escaping into the sheets."

She had to agree and moments later, he looked up to find an indescribable expression on her face, one that filled him with more joy than he thought one man could possibly contain.

"I love you, Rolph McKenzie," she whispered.

"I know," he said. "I love you too."

As he closed his eyes and kissed her, he heard a faint, musical tinkling, as if an unseen hand had brushed over a set of wind chimes. "What was that?" he asked, lifting his head.

"What was what?"

"You didn't hear a ringing sound?"

"I didn't hear a thing," she murmured. "Rolph, come back. Kiss me."

He did, adoring her, holding her close as she took him into her, enfolding him with her love. . . .

"I love you," she whispered sleepily some time later. As if in the echo of her words, he heard the sound of chimes again. He looked up in time to catch three golden bangles twirling gaily in the lamplight. As he stared in disbelief, they subsided and lay flat. That didn't happen, he told himself firmly. It didn't.

"I'll love you forever," Marian promised, and as he lay back, content, he heard again the clear, laughing sound of Gypsy music on an unseen wind.

"Well, I'll be damned," he murmured, laughing softly.

"Only a person with a Gypsy heart? *Me*?"

"What's that?" Marian asked.

"Nothing," he said. "Just planning a honeymoon, love. A long one."

THE EDITOR'S CORNER

For the best in summertime reading, look no further than the six superb LOVESWEPTs coming your way. As temperatures soar, what better way is there to escape from it all than by enjoying these upcoming love stories?

Barbara Boswell's newest LOVESWEPT is guaranteed to sweep you away into the marvelous world of high romance. A hell raiser from the wrong side of the tracks, Caleb Strong is back, and no red-blooded woman can blame Cheyenne Whitney Merit for giving in to his STRONG TEMPTATION, LOVESWEPT #486. The bad boy who left town years ago has grown into one virile hunk, and his hot, hungry kisses make "good girl" Cheyenne go wild with longing. But just as Caleb burns with desire for Cheyenne, so is he consumed by the need for revenge. And only her tender, healing love can drive away the darkness that threatens their fragile bond. A dramatic, thrilling story that's sensuously charged with unlimited passion.

The hero and heroine in SIZZLE by Marcia Evanick, LOVESWEPT #487, make the most unlikely couple you'll ever meet, but as Eben James and Summer Hudson find out, differences add spice to life . . . and love. Eben keeps his feet firmly planted in the ground, so when he discovers his golden-haired neighbor believes in a legendary sea monster, he's sure the gods are playing a joke on him. But there's nothing laughable about the excitement that crackles on the air whenever their gazes meet. Throwing caution to the wind, he woos Summer, and their courtship, at once uproarious and touching, will have you believing in the sheer magic of romance.

Welcome back Joan J. Domning, who presents the stormy tale of love lost, then regained, in RAINY DAY MAN, LOVESWEPT #488. Shane Halloran was trouble with a capital *T* when Merle Pierce fell hard for him in high school, but she never believed the sexy daredevil would abandon her. She devoted herself to her teenage advice column and tried to forget the man who ruined her for others. Now, more than twenty years later, fate intervenes, and Shane learns a truth Merle would have done anything to hide from him. Tempers flare but are doused in the sea of their long-suppressed passion for each other. Rest assured that all is forgiven between these two when the happy ending comes!

With her spellbinding sensuality, well-loved author Helen Mittermeyer captures A MOMENT IN TIME, LOVESWEPT #489. Hawk Dyhart acts like the consummate hero when he bravely rushes into the ocean to save a swimmer from a shark. Never mind that the shark turns out to be a diving flag and the swimmer an astonishingly beautiful woman who's furious at being rescued. Bahira Massoud is a magnificently exotic creature that Hawk must possess, but Bahira knows too well the danger of surrendering to a master of seduction. Still, she aches to taste the desire that Hawk arouses in her, and Hawk must walk a fine line to capture this sea goddess in his arms. Stunning and breathtaking, this is a romance you can't let yourself miss.

Let Victoria Leigh tantalize you with LITTLE SECRETS, LOVESWEPT #490. Ex-spy turned successful novelist I. J. Carlson drives Cassandra Lockland mad with his mocking glances and wicked come-ons. How could she be attracted to a man who provokes her each time they meet? Carlson sees the fire beneath her cool facade and stokes it with kisses that transform the love scenes in his books into sizzling reality. Once he breaches her defenses and uncovers her hidden fears, he sets out on a glorious campaign to win her trust. Will she be brave enough to face the risk of loving again? You'll be thoroughly mesmerized by this gem of a book.

Mary Kay McComas certainly lands her hero and heroine in a comedy of errors in ASKING FOR TROUBLE, LOVESWEPT #491. It all starts when Sydney Wiesman chooses Tom Ghorman from the contestants offered by the television show *Electra-Love*. He's smart, romantic, funny—the perfect man for the perfect date—but their evening together is filled with one disaster after another. Tom courageously sees them through each time trouble intervenes, but he knows this woman of his dreams can never accept the one thing in his life he can't change. Sydney must leave the safe and boring path to find the greatest adventure of all—a future with Tom. Don't miss this delectable treat.

FANFARE presents four truly spectacular books in women's popular fiction next month. Ask your bookseller for TEXAS! CHASE, the next sizzling novel in the TEXAS! trilogy by bestselling author Sandra Brown, THE MATCHMAKER by critically acclaimed Kay Hooper, RAINBOW by the very talented Patricia Potter, and FOLLOW THE SUN by ever-popular Deborah Smith.

Enjoy the summer with perfect reading from LOVESWEPT and FANFARE!

With every good wish,

Carolyn Nichols

Carolyn Nichols
Editor
LOVESWEPT
Bantam Books
666 Fifth Avenue
New York, NY 10103